Adriana's Family: A Novel

By

John Walters

Adriana's Family: A Novel

By

John Walters

Published by Astaria Books

Copyright 2021 by John Walters

This is a work of fiction. Any resemblance to actual persons places or events - except those in the public domain - is purely coincidental.

Contents

Part One: Adriana Gathers
Her Sisters and Brothers   1

Part Two: The Family Finds a Home   53

Part Three: Answers and Questions   123

End Notes   227

Part One: Adriana Gathers
Her Sisters and Brothers

I

From a strange and distant place where you have roamed, scattered, frightened, and far from the core that holds you together, you abruptly consolidate again into an entity capable of thought, capable of considering yourself as an individual. Your mind locks back into your body, and you can feel your body, somewhat at least.

You open your eyes. At first the brightness of the room is painful. The beige walls are bare. High up to your left is a single window blocked with bars. It is daytime; light streams in. To your right is a closed door. Behind you is a table full of instruments from which various tubes and wires extend to your body. A series of restrains binds you to the bed.

The restrains don't matter. You feel too weak to move anyway.

You have the impression that you should be able to remember why you are here, but you can't.

You remain dormant for an indeterminate period of time, content to be aware and to exist again as a person.

The door opens, and a woman enters. She is dressed in the white garb of a nurse.

You realize that you can recognize her as a *nurse* because you possess the gift of language. You have lost much but you have not lost everything. This comforts you.

"You're awake," says the woman. She glances at the instruments and then focuses on you. "I'm glad. I've been monitoring you from my station. We've been concerned."

You want to ask questions. Who has been concerned? Where are you? What has happened to you? How long have you been here? However, a thick tube leading into your mouth and down your throat prevents you from speaking.

"I know that you must have many questions," says the nurse. "They'll soon be answered. Please be patient. Recovery will take time."

Periods of consciousness and unconsciousness commence during which you observe the passage of the days by the alternating light and darkness.

The ventilation tube is removed. The nurse helps you sip water. For awhile your throat is too sore for you to attempt speaking. When you do, the nurse cautions you not to exert yourself. She says that she is not authorized to answer your questions, and that you have to wait.

One day an older woman in a plain gray pantsuit enters your room and sits in the chair next to your bed.

By this time, the restraints have been removed and your head and shoulders are propped up by several pillows. You still haven't commenced eating solid food, but you are able to drink water on your own.

"I'm the supervisor of this facility," she says. "Your name is Adriana. You are here because you experienced a severe traumatizing injury. It caused you to lose your memory. It may take time for you to get it back. In the meantime, we are going to assist you with neuropsychological and physical rehabilitation."

"What happened?" you whisper.

"We will explain everything when we think you are ready. In the meantime, please cooperate with your therapists so that you can recover more quickly."

You want to object, to insist, to remonstrate, but you realize that you haven't the strength. Not yet. At least you know who you are. That's something. Your name is Adriana.

The retraining of your body and mind commences. It takes the forms of massages, gently guided stretches, and exercises that gradually build up your strength. It also involves prolonged sessions in front of a monitor watching all sorts of disparate videos that don't seem to be related to one another and one-on-one interactions with a clinician. Her questions don't make any sense to you but you try to answer them as best you can. You inwardly celebrate when you take your first steps, when you first manage to swallow and digest semi-solid food, and when you formulate a coherent enough concept of reality that you manage to hold yourself together as a person.

You still don't remember anything from before you awakened in your bed, in your room, in this facility, but from the input you are receiving you construct a picture of the world outside. It is reeling from a devastating disaster. Many of the survivors in the nearby city are as disoriented as you are and are trying to recover and restore some semblance of normalcy. There is not much organization, not much leadership, and what little there is has consolidated into isolated units that for the most part are cut off from each other. Like this facility.

On the supervisor's next visit, you sit up and face her across a table. You ask her again, "What happened?"

"We were attacked," she says.

"By whom?"

"We don't know. Whoever the enemy was, we lost. For some reason our assailants didn't press their advantage. They defeated us and then left us alone to pick up the pieces."

"Who am I?"

"You're Adriana."

You stare pointedly at the supervisor.

"You have a family," she says. "We don't know where the rest of them are, but you can find them."

"How?"

"You have a gift of knowledge. You just know."

You shake your head. "I don't know anything except what you have shown me."

"We've held this information back. It's covered now. If we peel away the protection it's going to hurt for awhile like an open wound. But you'll know where they are. Maybe not all at once. Maybe one by one. We don't know."

"I have a family," you say. It's hard to make sense of the words. You know what a family is in an academic sense but you register none of the emotions that such a discovery should provoke.

"You don't understand now," says the supervisor, "but you will soon. And when you do, we want you to locate your brothers and sisters and bring them here. They have been lost but you can find them."

"When?"

"We think that you're ready now. You're physically strong enough, and you have regained enough orientation to make your way about safely on the outside."

"If I find them, I'll be home. Why don't I just stay there?"

"Your brothers and sisters are scattered. They're not all in one place. Once you return here with them, then we'll show you where home is."

"You know where it is? Why don't you tell me now?"

"It's not time yet. You'll have to trust us."

You don't really want to trust them but you don't have a choice. At the moment you are cocooned in their reality, and it is the only reality of which you are aware.

After the supervisor leaves, the nurse leads you down a pale corridor you have never entered before to a large well-lit room in which two people swathed in blue face masks and spotless white garments wait for you. They stand on either side of an austere bed or operating table.

One of them beckons.

You come closer while your nurse remains outside the door.

"Lie down on the table, please."

You comply.

Restraining straps are applied, and then two metallic hemispheres are placed on either side of your head. They are cool, smooth, and barely touch you.

"Relax. You're going to feel some tension. When you do, don't be alarmed. The discomfort will pass."

You close your eyes. An attendant places something in your mouth. "This will keep your teeth from grinding." For awhile nothing happens and you wonder if the supervisor was exaggerating about the pain or if perhaps this is not the procedure that she was talking about. After several minutes, though, it begins. You feel increasing pressure on your head, but not on the skin and skull that make up your physical head; instead, the pressure is on your mind, as if your psyche is something substantial that can be touched and squeezed. At first it merely feels odd, and then it is distressing, and then it hurts. The initial pain is manageable, and then it becomes less so, and then your head is being compressed so tightly that you imagine that it will soon burst. Just at the point when you consider the pressure intolerable, it stabilizes.

And then the removal starts. You don't know what exactly is being removed, but the sensation is similar to skin being peeled off layer by layer, slowly and meticulously. You want to scream but the mouth guard prevents it. You can do nothing but endure it. You can't even pass out; the trauma is too severe.

The procedure reaches a point at which there are no more layers to peel. Instead, there is a raw and open wound. It's like an exposed nerve. If anyone touches it, the pain will be unbearable. However, you abruptly realize that no one else can touch that spot. Only you have access to it. The procedure is over; creating this opening, this vulnerability, has been its objective.

You allow your muscles, which have become tight in reaction to the pain, to relax.

The attendants remove the metallic hemispheres and loosen the straps.

You remain motionless, allowing your body and mind to calm down.

It is as the supervisor has said. You have not regained your lost memories, but you have become aware of your family. Most of them exist as vague, barely discernible suggestions, but there is one clearer than the rest: your sister. Her presence is strong. She is nearby; you must go to her.

II

Andy is stalking a lizard sunning on a rock. The reptile's mottled gray skin blends with its surroundings but Andy knows exactly where it is. He creeps through open spaces and under bushes with large flat shiny green leaves. Slowly, slowly, ever so slowly he advances, with great restraint, barely able to contain his excitement. This is not how he prefers to do it; he would rather bound forward, running and leaping, barking furiously. And ideally he would not be doing it for survival but for fun, and when the excitement was over he would receive praises and caresses and snacks. But he has been on his own for weeks now, subsisting on bits of food he can salvage from garbage bins. He has tried hunting squirrels, rabbits, mice, and other small mammals but has so far been unsuccessful.

When he can stand the suspense no longer Andy rushes forward. It's not even close. The lizard scurries into a crack under the rock, and Andy expends his frustration futilely digging into the dry ground.

But wait! What does he smell and hear and see? It's a human person coming down the path. His first instinct is to growl, but he doesn't pay any attention to that. Instead, he runs to meet her, barking and wagging his tail.

I'm Andy! I'm Andy! Hello, hello!

The woman stops as Andy cavorts before her.

"Hello, Andy. I'm Adriana."

Andy stops jumping, although he can't prevent his tail from continuing to wag furiously. *You understand me? You understand Andy?*

"Yes."

How? This has never happened before. I understand humans, but humans don't understand back.

"I don't know." She kneels down so she's closer to his height. He tries to lick her face but she backs away, so he licks her hand instead. "I'm only supposed to sense my family."

Then I am your family. I, Andy. Family.

"I don't think so. My family has human members."

I used to be part of a family with human members. Now I am part of yours.

Adriana smiles and strokes Andy's head.

Yes, pet Andy. Pet Andy. Andy was lonely, but not now.

"What happened to your family?

Gone. Gone in the fires. Left Andy alone.

Adriana sighs. "So now you want to be part of my family, do you?"

Yes, yes. Please. Please. Andy will obey. Andy will help.

"Are you hungry, Andy?"

Yes, yes. Very hungry. Hard to find food. Humans fed Andy before.

Adriana takes off her backpack, pulls out a plastic packet, and tosses Andy a piece of dried meat. Andy avidly devours it and wags his tail expectantly. Adriana throws him another piece, puts the packet away, and hoists the backpack onto her shoulders. "That's all for now," she says. "So you want to come with me?"

Yes please. Yes please.

"Maybe you *are* a member of the family after all. A day ago I didn't even know that I had a family."

Yes. I am family. Where do we go?

"I have to find my brothers and sisters. Come on then, Andy. Let's go."

III

She awakens shortly before dawn on her thin foam floor mat. The flimsy blanket they gave her does not keep out the chill, but when she asked Sister Superior for another one, she was told that deprivation leads to saintliness. For several mornings after she arrived at the convent, Sister Josephine, the disciplinarian, came around at sunrise to rouse her, but now her physiology has adapted to the routine, the only routine she knows. She remains motionless, eyes closed, and tries to pray. Curious that she still finds it so difficult. Sister Sarah, the novitiate instructor, insists that it will get easier once she remembers how. For now, though, the past is a blank, as is the future.

She rises and uses the bucket that serves as a chamber pot. She can do nothing more until Sister Josephine comes along and opens the door of her cell. It's locked for her protection, they say, even though she hasn't yet been aware of any threat.

In the absence of prayer, what does one do when alone in the chilly darkness?

She crosses over to the window and looks out at the clear star-strewn night sky. An edge of it is deep blue instead of black: a harbinger of the approaching day. She grasps one of the rusting bars and quietly hums a tune that she doesn't quite remember.

Below the level of her vision she hears a *clack* as if something is placed against the wall. And then she hears the melody that she has been humming repeated back to her. A moment later, a face appears at the window.

She supposes that she would be expected to cry out, but she doesn't.

The woman at the window puts her finger to her lips, signaling for silence. She uses a small hammer and chisel to chip away at the base of two of the bars. The old concrete crumbles easily, and in minutes the woman has pulled the bars aside and climbed into the room.

"Who are you?"

"My name is Adriana. Don't be afraid."

"I'm not afraid."

"What's your name?"

"They call me Rahab. I don't know what it was before, but I don't think it was that. They say the name reflects my sins, the ones that traumatized me so much that I lost my memory."

"No, that's not your name. Your real name is Celeste."

"How do you know that?"

"Because you're my sister."

"But we're not even the same color."

"Does it matter?"

"No. The women who live here all call themselves my sisters, but it's a formality; it's obvious they're not. With you it's different."

"I would have been here sooner, but when I came to the gate they wouldn't let me see you. They tried to recruit me. I had to find another way."

"How did you locate me?"

"I don't know. I just knew where you were. I have that ability. You're the first I've found, but you're not the only one. We have other brothers and sisters that are lost. Do you want to help me find them?"

"Yes."

Adriana takes off her back pack and reaches inside. "Here, I brought you a change of clothes."

"We'd better hurry," says Celeste. "The others will start waking up soon."

"Come on. There's a ladder below the window ledge. I'll go first."

At the base of the ladder Andy waits, hopping and panting and wagging his tail.

"This is Andy," says Adriana.

Our sister! Our sister! Can she hear me like you can?

"I don't think so," says Adriana.

"What did you say?" says Celeste.

"I was talking to the dog," says Adriana. "Come on. I'll explain on the way."

IV

How long has Digger been buried alive in this dark narrow tunnel far underground? He has no way of knowing. All he knows is that he is hungry and thirsty and exhausted and frightened. For a long time he cried out for help but now his throat hurts and he couldn't shout for help if he wanted to. Anyway, the passage is too narrow for adults to crawl through and Digger know that they won't risk sending another child down after him.

What circumstances brought him here? Digger can't remember too far back, but he recalls attempting to steal a piece of fruit from a roadside stall and getting caught. He was brought before a filthy, gruff-looking man who called himself a recruiter. The man asked Digger if he wanted to go to prison or he wanted to work for him. If he went to prison, he would rot behind bars and be abused every day; if he accepted the work he would have food and a warm dry bed and be safe from harassment. I need children like you, said the man. Small and thin, so that you can fit into places other people can't go. These collapsed buildings have essential food and supplies buried under them. You'll be performing a great service if you help us find these things. You'll be a hero.

Digger later found out that his employer didn't give away what he and the other children found; he bartered for weapons and other high-value items. Still, as long as Digger and the others did as they were told, the man kept his end of the bargain. He fed them and they slept together in a dormitory full of cots. It wasn't exactly the same as being in a family, but it was better than being alone out on the streets.

Most of the time Digger was ordered to wriggle through heaps of rubble and extract anything of worth he found. This time, however, his employer took him into a basement and then a subbasement of a building. The concrete foundation had cracked and there was a partially collapsed tunnel underneath.

I think there is a vault down there, the man said. I want you to go and find out. Here, take this. He switched on a flashlight and handed it to Digger. The flashlight let out a dim amber glow. Go on, then.

Eager to please, Digger squeezed his way through the crack and dropped onto the damp dirt beneath. For a short distance he could walk crouched down, and then he had to drop to his hands and knees and crawl. The passage seemed to have once been some sort of corridor, but the sides and ceiling had caved and it had all but filled in. The way became narrower and narrower until Digger was forced to inch his way forward on his elbows. He was reluctant to disappoint his employer so he kept going as long as he could. He reached a point, though, where he could proceed no further. In a slightly widened space he managed to turn around and was just about to commence crawling out when his foot kicked a wall and a mass of dirt crumbled and fell over his lower body. He frantically tried freeing himself but he couldn't move. He called for help but nobody came. He screamed as long as he could. He wept. He watched the faint glow of the flashlight dwindle and disappear.

He has remained here alone in the darkness for a long, long time, drifting in and out of consciousness, terrified that fierce slithery monsters might come and feed on him. The silence is as frightening as the utter blackness around him. He wonders if it would be better if he goes to sleep and never wakes up.

And then he hears a noise. Something is coming towards him through the tunnel. He can hear it breathing. He can hear the displacement of dirt and rubble as it crawls. Whatever it is, it's getting closer and closer.

Digger wants to scream, but his throat hurts too much; and anyway, he's too scared to scream. He waits in dread anticipation for the creature to commence feeding on him. The breathing and crawling noises get louder and louder. The thing is only inches away.

However, instead of biting him, it begins to lick his face.

It's a dog!

For some reason it seems very happy to have found him. Digger can sense its joy.

After a time it stops licking and starts digging where his body is buried. Digger can feel the packed dirt loosening. He tries to wriggle free. Slowly, slowly, as the dog digs, he manages to crawl forward inch by inch.

After Digger is no longer trapped, the dog licks his face again for a moment and then leads the way out. Digger cannot see the dog, but he can hear and sense him. Whenever Digger stops to rest, the dog stops too and waits until he hears Digger continue.

In this way they proceed through the darkness.

Far ahead, Digger sees a glimmer of light. It takes him a long time to reach it. When he does, he squeezes through the crack in the concrete to find two women waiting for him and the dog shaking the dirt out of his long black, gold, and white fur.

The women lie him down on a blanket with his head propped up with a pack.

I've found him! I've found him! Our brother, our brother! says Andy.

"Here," says Adriana.

Digger accepts the water and drinks deeply.

"Not so fast," says Adriana. "Sip it."

Digger drinks his fill, and as he does his fears subside and he calms down.

"I'm Adriana. This is Celeste, and that's Andy."

Andy wags his tail.

"What's your name?" says Celeste.

"They call me Digger."

"That's not your real name, though," says Adriana.

"How do you know?"

"Because you're our brother," says Adriana.

"But you two aren't even the same color."

"It doesn't matter," says Celeste.

"So what's my name, then?"

"It's Travis."

He looks at Adriana, and then at Celeste, and then at Andy, whose tail is still wagging furiously. "Okay, then."

V

After Derek finishes filling his pack with bricks and hoists it up to its position on his shoulders and back, he takes a brief look up. The sun has gone below the jagged skyline of broken buildings. This may be his last haul of the day. His hours are from sunup to sundown; lighting isn't

18

good enough at the construction sites or they'd probably keep him working on into the night. As it is, he is exhausted. All day he totes bricks from rubbish heaps to new building sites. He takes numerous brief breaks to smoke cigarettes laced with hashish and a slightly longer break to wolf down beans and bread. Otherwise he trudges methodically up and down the streets, one step after another, not thinking about much of anything really except when the day might end so he can collect his pay and then spend it on liquor and women.

Once one of the overseers got pushy trying to get him to move faster. Derek turned and without removing the pack from his back punched the man in the face. The man went down hard, blood spouting from his nose. That particular supervisor stays well away from Derek now, and the others let him walk at his own pace.

Derek reaches the site where bricklayers and cement mixers are preparing the foundations for a new building, and it is as he supposed. They are collecting the packs for the day. He lowers his to the ground and removes the materials he has been carrying. As he turns in his pack, he receives his money. He nods, and the payroll distributor nods in turn. That's the extent of the official transaction.

Although Derek is tired, he's in no mood to go back to the room in a warehouse he shares with a dozen or so other laborers. He is in the mood for entertainment. That's how it has been every day recently: he works, he gets paid, and then he spends most or all of the money. Sometimes he makes it back to his bed and sometimes he doesn't.

At a trough full of murky water he does a rudimentary job of washing his hands and face. He then retrieves his shirt from where it's been hanging in the storage shed, puts it on, and starts down a rubble-choked street towards the waterfront. Derek has helped to clear a path through this mess; it used to be all but impassible. He doesn't think about that, though; he doesn't think about much of anything.

At the end of the second block a cute little long-haired dog runs up to him barking and wagging its tail. Usually he doesn't pay much attention to dogs unless they attack. The ones he's encountered tend to be feral and run in packs. A few times he's had to fight them off with rocks and sticks. This one, though, is a friendly fellow. Derek crouches down and pets it while the dog jumps and licks and barks.

And then Derek is aware that a group of people have approached and they are observing him.

Derek straightens up and says, "Good evening, ladies. Are you for hire?"

"For hire?" says Celeste.

"No," says Adriana. "But we've been looking for you."

"The only ladies that seek me out are in business," says Derek. "If you're not one of those, then step aside. I'm on my way to get a drink."

Adriana pulls a small bottle out of one of her pockets and tosses it to him.

"Thanks." Derek twists the cap off and gulps down half the contents. He then screws the cap back on and puts the bottle in his own pocket. Neither of the women objects. "So... You say you've been looking for me?"

"That's right," says Adriana.

"Why?"

"You're our brother," says Adriana.

Derek looks at Adriana, and then Celeste, and then Travis. He chuckles and says, "How is that possible?"

"It just is," says Adriana. "You're our brother and we need you. So forget that debilitating job and your drinking and your whoring and come with us. We've got more family to find."

Derek starts to reach for the bottle and then hesitates. "I don't remember having a family," he says.

"None of us do," says Adriana, "except me. And I remember only a little, and only because I had some help. "But we're going to find the rest of our siblings, and then we're going home."

"Where is home?" says Derek.

"I don't know," says Adriana. "But someone has promised to help us find out."

"What's his name?" says Travis, pointing at Derek.

"Why don't you ask *me* what my name is?" says Derek.

Travis nods at Adriana. "Because she's probably going to change it."

"I'm not going to change it," says Adriana. "I already know what it is. It's Marcus."

"No it isn't," says Derek/Marcus.

"It has been until now. If you don't like it, then call yourself whatever you want."

Derek/Marcus ruminates for awhile. "I'm confused."

Adriana says, "We all are. Let's keep it simple. The only choices you need to make now are whether you believe us and whether you're going to join us. The rest we can work out on the way."

VI

The librarian can't remember her name, so she's been changing it every day and sometimes twice a day. At the moment she is Toni. She wanders the aisles between bookshelves, caressing the spines and sometimes taking down volumes and reading a page or two. She is aware on a visceral level that she has some sort of relationship with these books. She knows them. She knows them intimately; they are her friends. Somehow she has forgotten the details, but she is confident that eventually they will come back to her. In the meantime, she has set herself up as the guardian of knowledge. Several days ago a group of rowdy kids came in and made off with armloads of books. They intended to use them as kindling to start fires. The librarian couldn't let that happen, so she locked up all the windows and their shutters, bolted the doors, and for good measure braced the doors with heavy tables. The water still runs in the taps and there is food stored in the cafeteria, so she is prepared for a siege.

The sun has just set, and Toni breathes a sigh of relief. The nights have been quiet for the most part. Occasionally she spots flames from an upper story window, but none of the fires have been close. To avoid attracting attention she doesn't use lights except in the interior. She knows the building intimately; she can easily feel her way around the spacious public rooms. She fears the darkness outside, but not the darkness within the building. This is her space. She is at home here.

She sits facing a window on the second floor and watches light fade from the deep blue sky. Already a few stars have begun to appear. Street lamps in the city are so scattered and dim that they do not impede the glow of faraway celestial wonders.

Time to eat. Time to rest.

Toni stands and stretches.

And then she hears a knock on the door.

No. It can't be. She must have imagined it.

There it is again.

And voices calling out. She can't understand what they are saying.

Her first impulse is to hide in the cafeteria until they go away, but then she becomes curious. Who could these people be?

She steps quietly down the central stairs in the deep shadows of the main hall, makes her way to the front door, and listens.

A woman's voice calls out. "I know you can hear us. Please let us in."

There's something familiar about that voice... However, she said *us*. That means that others are with her. Toni feels threatened and remains silent.

A dog barks. It's not the savage, feral bark of the packs that run in the streets, though; it exudes friendliness and good will.

Toni is torn between the desire to yield to her loneliness and longing for companionship, which she has so far managed to suppress, and her resolve to maintain strict security.

"We've been looking for you," says the voice.

Toni blurts out, "Why? You don't even know me," and then realizes that she has given herself away.

"Don't be frightened. We don't mean you any harm."

At that moment something erupts inside Toni and she starts weeping. She doesn't care anymore about self-protection. She needs to open the door. She can't help it.

In her anxiety and impatience she fumbles with the bolts. When she swings half of the heavy double wooden door open, silhouetted against the dim yellow light of a solitary street lamp she sees two women, a large man, a boy, and...

The dog runs in and commences wagging his tail and licking Toni's hand.

The woman who has been calling out says, "That's Andy. This is Celeste, Travis, and Marcus. And I'm Adriana."

Toni is momentarily speechless.

Andy continues to leap about and lick her hands.

Finally Toni says, "Would you like to come inside?" After they do she adds, "Maybe we'd better lock the doors again."

The man called Marcus slips the bolts back into place and checks to make sure they are secure.

"This is hard to explain," says Adriana.

Our sister! Our sister! says Andy.

"You're our sister," says Celeste.

"We're your family," says Travis, and smiles.

"My family?"

"Yeah, it takes some getting used to," says Marcus.

"But I don't have..." Toni hesitates because she doesn't know *what* she has. She can't remember anything beyond the last week or two.

"Do you know what *her* name is?" says Travis.

"Yes," says Adriana.

"What is it?" says Toni, knowing that her name isn't really Toni.

"Your name is Sage."

"Sage," she repeats with a reflective inward-focused gaze.

Sage! Sage! says Andy, barking and leaping around with joy.

"You need to quiet down now, Andy," says Adriana.

He stops barking but his tail keeps wagging.

"Would you like to come upstairs?" says Sage. "We can turn on the lights there."

In the cafeteria the central dining table is piled with books. Sage moves some of them to the side so they can all sit down.

"Do you read these?" says Marcus.

"I love to read," says Sage. "That's why I've been trying to guard the library."

Marcus idly opens one of the volumes, squints, looks closer, and then exclaims, "I can read too!" He looks up shamefacedly. "I thought I was dumb. I can't remember anything except for hauling bricks and drinking. It didn't occur to me that I might have done something different before." He skims the page and chuckles. "This is good. This is very good."

"Books are worlds that you can carry around with you," says Sage.

Adriana says, "We need to keep looking for our family. I think there's just one more member we haven't found. We have to leave soon."

"But it isn't safe to walk around outside at night," says Sage.

"We'll be all right," says Marcus. "Don't worry."

Sage smiles. "I'm not worried. I'm not. But what about the books? We have to protect them."

"I know what we can do," says Travis. "You all go out the door and then I'll lock it up. You can show me how. And then I'll go out a window upstairs and climb down. I'm a good climber."

VII

The already-brisk wind has increased in intensity, and at the base of the bluff rough seas smash against jagged rocks.

The artist turns off the light in her studio. This residence, which was constructed to simulate a lighthouse, had been abandoned because of the confusion, and the artist has moved in and claimed it. The upstairs is a single large circular room reached via a spiral staircase. Downstairs are several small bedrooms, a bathroom, a kitchen, and a dining room/living room area with large picture windows facing the ocean. On the long wooden dining table she has set out plates, bowls, cutlery, glasses, loaves of bread, and bottles of wine. In the kitchen a large pot of stew simmers. It is not fresh; it is assembled from the contents of cans, but nevertheless it gives off a fine savory smell that wafts from the kitchen throughout the rest of the house.

The feast has been prepared. Where are the guests?

The artist opens the door to the balcony that surrounds the circular upstairs room, steps out into the strong breeze, and closes the door behind her. Holding the rail, she circles around until she can see the road that winds up the hill from the city. No lights illuminate it, but the moon, which is nearly full, shines periodically from behind swift-moving clouds. At first she sees nothing on the road. The metropolis itself, once resplendent with the intensity of its lights, now manifests its presence with intermittent sputters of feeble glows.

She thought that her guests would be close by now. It does not even enter her thoughts that they might not come.

Wait! Yes, there they are! Five people and a dog. She has not prepared anything for the dog, but the former owners of this residence kept pets; she supposes she will find something that it will like.

She makes her way back around to the door. When she closes it the harsh rushing noise of the wind stops, and the silence is like a benediction. Crossing the darkened studio, she steps down the stairs into the warm light of the dining area. After checking the food in the kitchen, she turns on the light in the entrance hallway and opens the front door.

They have come to the front gate at the end of the long driveway. A tall man is working the metal bolt loose. The gate opens, they file through, and the man secures the gate again.

The people walk slowly up the driveway, but the dog runs full speed.

The artist chuckles and stoops down. She hugs the dog as it frantically licks her face.

By the time she stands, the others have arrived.

"Welcome," says the artist. "Please come in."

"You've been expecting us?" says Celeste.

"Yes. I didn't know who it would be, but I knew someone would come."

In the entryway, Adriana introduces everyone.

The artist says, "My name is Vera."

"What's her real name?" says Travis with a grin.

"That's it," says Adriana. "She's got it right."

Travis looks at Vera with astonishment.

Vera leads them into the room where the feast has been prepared. "Everything is ready," she says. "You can wash up in there."

While everyone takes turns in the bathroom, Vera looks for something that Andy can eat. She finds a bag of dried dog food and pours some into a ceramic bowl. "I hope he'll like this," she says, as she sets it on the floor next to another bowl filled with water.

"He says it's great," Adriana says. "He used to eat something similar when he lived with his former family."

"You can communicate with him?"

"Yes. I'm the only one that can, though."

"I almost feel like I can sense his thoughts, but it's not in words. More like empathy, I suppose."

"That's how it is for some people. So... How is it that you were able to anticipate our arrival, Vera?"

"I... It just comes to me. I'll show you tomorrow. For now, let's eat."

By this time the others have sat down at the table. Vera carries out the large steaming pot and sets it down on a hot pad. She starts ladling out stew while Adriana opens two wine bottles.

This supper that they share in the abandoned lighthouse-shaped residence is surreal in its simple joy. They chat and laugh. They share stories with Vera about how they have found each other throughout the day. Vera tells of coming upon the house, of moving in, and of working on a large painting upstairs.

"Can we see it?" says Travis.

"We should wait until morning," says Vera. "The light will be better. For tonight, you can all sleep comfortably and well."

Celeste asks Adriana, "Are there more sisters and brothers to be found?"

"I don't think so," says Adriana. "I think this is all of us."

Vera says, "How do you know?"

Adriana shakes her head. "I don't know how I know. I just know."

In a hesitant manner Marcus says, "In the library I found out that I could read. I keep having feelings and flashes that I know more than I can remember. Why is that?"

"I don't know for sure," says Adriana, "but in the facility where I woke up, I went through some kind of treatment. It hurt a lot, but it was only after that when I knew how to find you all. They asked me to find you and bring you back. Maybe they can awaken something in you too."

"Someone told you to find us?" says Sage.

"Yes."

"How do we know we can trust them?" says Celeste. "What if they're manipulating you like my overseers manipulated me at the convent?"

"We don't know for sure," says Adriana. "All we can do is take it step by step and try to sense right from wrong. It worked so far though, didn't it? It brought us together. You're all here because you want to be, aren't you? Any of you at any time can walk out the door and go your own way."

Adriana, Celeste, Travis, Marcus, Sage, and Vera all looked at each other.

Andy, having finished his repast, observed them, wagging his tail.

"Whatever we were before, now we are somehow a family," says Sage. "I don't think any of us are going to leave."

They all nodded and mumbled assent.

"The people at the facility sent me out to find you," says Adriana, "but that doesn't mean we have to go back there. We can do whatever we want. Let's wait until tomorrow and then we can all decide together what we're going to do."

*   *   *

Adriana awakens in semi-darkness, but she can see from the edges of light around the curtains that the sun has already come up. She is on the bottom half of a bunk bed. Above her sleeps Celeste, and across from them on a single bed sleeps Sage.

Adriana gets up and dresses quietly.

Vera is already active in the kitchen. She gives Adriana a cup of coffee and a piece of bread slathered with peanut butter. Adriana sits alone at the dining table as she eats and drinks. The view from the picture windows dominates the room. Beyond the bluff, sunlight sparkles on blue ocean waters that stretch interminably to the horizon.

After Adriana finishes her breakfast, takes her cup to the kitchen sink, and after using the bathroom, she stands and watches the way the shifting ocean waters create ever-changing light patterns.

Vera comes up behind her. "There's something I'd like to show you," she says.

Vera leads Adriana up the spiral staircase to the circular room. Multiple skylights flood the area with sunlight. The curved walls are solid and windowless. The base paint is white, but about two-thirds of the circumference up to as high as Vera can reach has been covered over with an elaborate multicolored mural.

"I've been working on this since I got here," says Vera, "from early morning and for as long as the natural light has lasted. I've worked until my arms were so tired that I could barely hold them up. I have begrudged stopping to eat or to use the toilet. Something has compelled me. I haven't been able to help myself. Until last night I had no idea why I was doing it, but now I think I understand, at least a little."

The painting is episodic; one scene blends into the next. It begins with a view of the unbroken city. Stick-like figures of men and women go about their business in the streets and in the shops. Cars ply the roadways and boats cruise the harbor. The sky is slightly overcast, as if rain is imminent, but not as if a storm is approaching.

A thrill rushes through Adriana as she contemplates the intact city with its myriad inhabitants. She must have once lived as one of them in such a place, but she cannot remember having done so. The past has vanished behind a misty wall that she is yet unable to penetrate. This image, though, has verisimilitude; how has Vera managed to recall it and preserve it?

The next scene shows the same city, but this time visitors have arrived. Vehicles fly through the cloud cover; visitors descend on light beams that directly touch specific people. Some seem to receive the visitors, while others reject them. The city, meanwhile, is awash in waves of multicolored brightness and shadow.

Next, some people withdraw from view and others become enraged and commence deeds of destruction. The individuals have evolved from stick figures to more complex characters with individualistic features, although all the expressions are either fear or rage.

After this scene, the next is quieter. It is here that Adriana notices in a corner of the painting five people and a dog taking a winding road at twilight toward a lighthouse-shaped building on a bluff.

"How did you..?" she begins, and then stops. This is not the end of the mural. There is another scene after this one; it goes on. "But this hasn't even happened yet," she says.

Vera says, "When I painted the scene of all of you approaching the house, that hadn't happened yet either. I became inspired; I imagined it, and then I drew and colored it. But I *was* expecting you. I had the food ready, remember? I can't explain it."

"Maybe we should stay here while you paint some more," says Adriana. "We may get a better idea of what's going on."

"I don't think that's how it works," says Vera. "That's not what this next part shows."

"But is that a prediction or a suggestion?"

"I don't know."

As Adriana and Vera descend the steps, the others begin to emerge from their rooms.

Andy runs up to Adriana, tail wagging furiously. *Andy is here! Andy is here! Happy, happy! Andy is happy!*

Adriana stoops down and strokes Andy's head. "Good morning, Andy."

Vera goes off to the kitchen to help people find coffee and food. Soon they all sit around the table watching sunlight tickle the ocean.

"What do we do now?" says Celeste. "You said last night that you thought there was no one else in our family to find. Is that true?"

Adriana says, "Until Vera, whenever I found one of you, I would immediately sense the next one.

I don't have that sensation anymore. I think we're complete."

Travis says, "But we're not really a family, are we? We're all different ages, and we don't look anything alike."

"I can't answer your questions," says Adriana. "I just don't know. To find out these things, we might have to go back to the facility I started from."

"It could be dangerous," says Sage. "They might try to control us, to use us."

"We can stay here," says Vera. "I've been safe here."

Adriana says, "But if we stay here, we won't learn anything. We won't grow. We'll just survive."

"Survival was enough before," says Marcus.

"That was when you were alone," says Adriana. "Now we have each other. We can help each other; we can protect each other. We can do more."

"Let's rest for a day," says Celeste. "It's the first time I've been free from Mother Superior since I can remember."

"And I'm free of the tunnels," says Travis.

"And I'm free of my job," says Marcus.

"And I'm free of the library," says Sage.

I'm free! I'm free! And I'm happy! says Andy.

VIII

Adriana doesn't remember the facility being so massive and white and austere. A stark smooth ten-foot-high wall surrounds it. They stand in front of the gate but have not yet touched the intercom.

"I don't like this place," says Celeste.

"Neither do I," says Marcus.

The others mumble similar opinions.

"I agree with you," says Adriana. "But we've come this far." She stoops down to talk to Andy. "Stay very quiet," she says. "Don't let anyone know that we can communicate. Listen for me and come quickly if I call you."

Yes! says Andy. *Yes! Yes!*

Adriana presses the button next to the speaker. "Hello? This is Adriana. I've come back. I've brought my family with me."

The speaker crackles and buzzes, but no one answers.

After a moment, the metal gate glides aside with a rumble and a screech.

Adriana, Celeste, Travis, Marcus, Sage, Vera, and Andy follow a long path past landscaped gardens to a large open glass door. Outside stands a woman clad in white; Adriana recognizes her as one of the nurses who tended to her when she was recuperating.

The nurse smiles, with her mouth at least. "So nice to see you. Come this way, please." She leads them into a reception area and bids them relax on the comfortable couches, and then she exits the room.

The family members look at one another.

Minutes pass.

The supervisor enters along with several other people. "You've returned," she says to Adriana. "How wonderful."

"This is my family," says Adriana. She introduces them. "You said you'd tell us where our home is. That's why we've come."

"Yes of course." The supervisor notices Andy, who is sitting quietly at Adriana's feet. "What is that dog doing here?"

"He's ours," says Adriana. "A family pet."

"You should know that pets are not allowed in this facility," says the supervisor.

"We'll leave, then," says Adriana. "Just tell us where to go to find our home."

"We will," says the supervisor. "But first we want to be sure that everyone is healthy. That's why these people are here: so they can escort you to examination rooms."

"We're fine," says Adriana. "We want to be on our way."

"Adriana," says the supervisor. "All of you. Listen to me. Since the war there have been epidemics of diseases. You might be carrying something dangerous that you don't even know you have. It's better to be safe."

"I don't mind an examination," says Sage.

"Whatever *you* say," says Travis, looking at Adriana and not at the supervisor.

"How long will it take?" says Adriana.

"Not more than an hour," says the supervisor. "When you're finished, you can have a nice meal. If you want, you can stay here for the night and have a fresh start in the morning."

"We'll see about that later," says Adriana. She nods, and the others leave with the attendants. Some are male and some female, but all are attractive, healthy, and have smiles set in place as if by internal wire frames.

When they are alone in the room with the final attendant, the supervisor tells Adriana, "You have done well."

"Thank you."

"You need to undergo an examination too."

"First tell me where our home is."

"When the time is right I will tell you."

"The right time is now."

The supervisor pursed her lips. "No it isn't. Please go with this man. Now."

"No. You're not being honest with me, are you?"

The attendant starts forward, but the supervisor puts up her hand and he stops. "I haven't told you anything that's a lie," she says. "We were attacked. Our enemies were not of this world. They infiltrated us; by that I mean that they literally got inside some of us. Inside you. You had forgotten who you were. We rescued you. We cleaned you out. They had done something to you so that you could recognize them, so we sent you out to find other infected people."

"My family."

"They're not your family. They are alien-infested humans who require cleansing."

"And our home?"

"I'm sorry. You have no other home than this place here."

"This is no home."

"It can be. It will be. We can work out the details later. For now you need to go with this man so we can verify that you are not infected."

"Can my dog come with me?"

The supervisor looks as if she is about to refuse; after considering Adriana's expression, she thinks better of it. "All right. If he doesn't make a fuss."

Adriana follows the attendant down a hallway. Andy follows Adriana. They arrive in a small room that looks similar to the one in which Adriana spent her recovery.

"Please lie down on the bed," says the attendant.

Before she complies, Adriana tells Andy to wait in the corner. He curls himself into a bundle and rests his head on his paws.

"Obedient, isn't he?" says the attendant.

"Yes," says Adriana.

The attendant quickly applies straps to Adriana's chest midriff, ankles, and wrists. He then cinches them tighter and tighter until Adriana winces.

"Is this really necessary?" she says.

"We don't want you hurting yourself," says the attendant.

Adriana remembers the pain of the procedure that opened her awareness so that she could detect her family. She doesn't want to go through that again.

Then the attendant pulls two metallic hemispheres out of a drawer. "No," says Adriana. "No. I don't want to do this."

"You don't have much choice, do you?" says the attendant. As he puts the hemispheres in place beside her skull the attendant leans close enough so that Adriana can smell the coffee on his breath. "It's going to hurt. A lot. I hear that the mortality rate is high in these procedures. If it was up to me, we wouldn't bother with this so-called purging and rehabilitation. I lost people I loved during the wars. We should kill you all as soon as we find you. In fact, since everyone else is busy taking care of your friends, I think I can get away with a bit of overloading here. Let's see how much frying your brain can take."

*　　*　　*

You break down and cry then, but not for yourself. You are concerned about your family, the ones you've come to love. They have trusted you and followed you here, right into a trap. Straining against the straps is useless; he really did cinch them tight. Calling for Andy won't help either. He's a small dog and is no match for the powerful attendant. He would fight willingly, but he would only get himself killed.

You wish that you could somehow call out to the others to get them to flee, but you realize that it's already too late. They will be strapped down too by now; they will have horrible tortuous metallic devices placed around their skulls. They may already be feeling the pressure.

As you feel it. It comes on stronger and faster this time, like your psyche is an eggshell being squeezed in a vise. The attendant did not bother to give you a mouth guard this time. You grind your teeth, and then you scream from the pain. Somewhere in the periphery of your consciousness you hear Andy barking. The pressure increases. Something like a white-hot scalpel touches your mind. It goes straight to the wound with the raw nerve endings that was opened last time, the wound that is still there and hasn't healed, the wound that opened something that brought you awareness of the location of your family members.

The scalpel is ready to cut.

You prepare to lose your loved ones and your mind.

And then there they all are again, not one by one but all at once. You can sense them and they can sense you. Celeste and Travis and Marcus and Sage and Vera. And Andy. Yes, Andy is there too.

You wonder if this facility has ever conducted this procedure on so many people all at once before. You think not, or they might have gotten the same result. Or maybe yes, momentarily, but the procedure then killed their consciousness of it.

The visitors are lodged within each one of you. You are aware of them too. They are the ones making this interaction possible. It is a survival mechanism. Your family unit is not a human entity; the visitors have created it. But it is real. You all are no longer merely human, and the visitors are no longer merely visitors. Together you are something different. Something more.

*   *   *

A voice erupts from within Adriana and also, she realizes, within the other members of her family. It somehow translates into language she can understand.

We meant you no harm. Our vehicles malfunctioned. Our corporeal husks became damaged. We escaped destruction by abandoning ship. Our parts were scattered, but you have reunited us. We are whole again. We will not threaten your autonomy as long as you stay together.

"But we're trapped," shouts Adriana. "We're in danger."

The inner voice does not respond.

The attendant, however, leans over Adriana and says, "What's that you say? You're in danger? I'll say you're in danger, and so is that damned dog of yours. We should have killed him straightaway." He opens a drawer and pulls out a full hypodermic syringe. "This is what we use if you're belligerent or threatening. It's lethal. I'm not sure who to use it on first, you or your dog." He lunges towards Andy, who scurries under the bed. The bed is on rollers, so it moves easily as the attendant pushes it aside. The wires leading to the metallic hemispheres are short, though, so the mechanism disengages and falls off of Adriana's head. The attendant chases Andy around the room, shoving the bed with strapped-down Adriana this way and that while Andy barks and runs and manages to always stay a few steps away. And then...

Adriana has a feeling that everything slows down and that the random chaos momentarily gives way to some sort of guidance or control. From where or whom she isn't sure, but she wonders if it has something to do with the voice she just heard.

The attendant stumbles and falls flat on his face. The syringe he is carrying impales him and injects its load into his chest. He lies motionless on the floor, not breathing.

"Andy," says Adriana. "Andy, come and help me."

Andy jumps up onto the bed and works on one of the straps binding Adriana's wrists. It is tight, but Andy patiently chews, grips, and pulls until it comes loose.

Once one wrist is out, Adriana is easily able to free herself.

"We have to find the others," says Adriana.

Andy can help!

"I know you can. But wait. I don't know if we can overcome all the attendants. I have an idea." Adriana pulls another deadly loaded hypodermic syringe from the drawer. "Do you think you can find the supervisor?"

Yes, yes! says Andy. *I remember her scent.*

"Let's go."

As it turns out, the facility isn't as large as it looks on the outside. There is a large central hallway. On one side of it are patients' quarters and examination rooms, and on the other are laboratories and administrative offices. Several of the doors to the examination rooms are closed, and Adriana senses her brothers and sisters behind them. They are unharmed, at least for the moment, but some of them are in pain.

"Where is she?" whispers Adriana.

Here. She is in here.

Adriana knocks on the door. When the supervisor opens it and leans out, Adriana grabs her arm, twists it behind her back, and presses the point of the needle against the supervisor's neck. "Do you know what this is?"

The supervisor nods.

"You're going to help me free my family."

The supervisor says, "You're making a mistake. They're... You're dangerous. You all are. We're here to help you."

"Yes," says Adriana. "You're going to help me." She pulls the supervisor out into the hallway.

Adriana can sense which of her brothers and sisters is behind each door. She frees Marcus first because he is the biggest and strongest, and then locks the attendant that was guarding him in the room. She then sets the others free one by one, and in the final room, in which Travis had been kept, she locks the supervisor in with Travis's attendant.

"What happened?" says Travis.

"These were bad people," says Adriana. "They were trying to hurt us. They were trying to make us forget we are a family."

"Let's leave, then," says Sage.

"Yes, we'll leave," says Adriana. "We'll go far away from here so they can't find us. But first we have to damage this facility so they can't hurt other people like they hurt us."

They individually escort each attendant and the supervisor to the cafeteria, which is an interior room with no windows and a solid door. Once all the personnel are locked up, Adriana divides the family into two groups of three. "We'll smash all the machines in the examination rooms and the equipment in the laboratories," she says. "Destroy any records you find too. And maybe we can shut down their source of power. But don't start any fires. We don't want to hurt the staff we've captured. Someone will come along eventually and let them out."

"But they hurt us," says Travis. "Why shouldn't we hurt them?"

"Because we're better than that," says Vera. "You can't let the bad behavior of others be an example for your own."

How can Andy help?

"You keep watch, Andy," says Adriana. "Warn us if you see or hear anyone coming. Now let's do this quickly. We don't know when they have changes of shift."

Marcus, Sage, and Vera take the side of the hall with the examination rooms. They enter each room in turn, break apart the mental probes, and use any heavy objects that they find to reduce them to fragments. They also empty cabinets and smash any bottles, vials, or syringes they find.

Andy runs up and down the hall from the front entrance to the back entrance of the facility watching, sniffing, and listening.

Adriana, Celeste, and Travis topple lab equipment, rip wires out of it, and pummel it with metal bars.

When they enter the supervisor's office, though, Adriana says, "Wait," before they destroy anything. "I want to see what's here."

She sits down at the desk in front of the computer and taps a few keys on the keyboard. The screen lights up, but it asks for a password. She opens drawers and pulls out papers and notebooks. One of these appears to be a logbook of patients admitted to the facility. Most of the entries are without names; they are listed merely as subjects with numbers. There are a few names, though, and Adriana starts skimming through the pages looking for hers.

And then she pauses. Does she really need to know where she came from? She can discern from the log that this facility has been in operation for quite some time. A major cataclysm happened, yes, but it didn't happen yesterday. Whatever was lost has already been lost. If in the past Adriana and her brothers and sisters had other families, those families are gone. What's the use of dredging up old information that cannot possibly be of use under the present circumstances? The idea is to venture forth and build the new world, not dwell in the remnants of the old.

The thought drifts through Adriana's awareness that perhaps the visitor within her is putting these ideas in her mind. Is she being manipulated? And then she considers the totality of her family, all seven members - fourteen in fact if you include the visitors - and the word *symbiosis* comes to her. No one entity is in control. They work together to thrive and grow.

Onward, then. Into the future.

Adriana stands up. She picks up the computer and throws it onto the floor. "Let's destroy as much as we can," she says. That machine chews up paper. We'll shred the documents. Come on, let's hurry. I want to get out of here as fast as we can."

When the six of them and Andy regroup in the hallway, Sage says, "They can probably repair everything and start this up again."

"We can't help that," says Adriana.

"They'll capture others. They'll hurt them," says Travis. "Isn't there anything more we can do to stop them?"

"We're not going to hurt them," says Adriana. "We can't be like that."

"This may not be their only location," says Vera. "There may be more of them in other places."

"If there are, we'll try to avoid them," says Adriana. "What else can we do? In the meantime, we need to go."

They head for the front door and exit into bright sunlight.

"Look over there," says Marcus. "It looks like a garage. Maybe they have vehicles."

"We shouldn't steal from them," says Celeste.

"What do we owe them?" says Travis. "They might have killed us, and they wouldn't have cared."

"I agree with Travis," says Adriana. "We need to move as quickly as possible, and the rules have changed. Let's check it out."

They enter the garage through a side door. Within are four navy blue minivans covered with veneers of dust. Each has driver and passenger seats in front and two rows of seats in back.

"They don't appear to be in very good shape," says Sage. "Come to think of it, I don't remember seeing any working vehicles in the city."

"Does anyone even know how to drive?" says Vera.

Marcus has rested his hands on the hood of one of the vans. "I can, I think," he says, "but we need the keys."

"Over here," says Celeste. In a corner is a desk, and above it is a board with hooks holding the keys.

Marcus opens and starts one van but expresses dissatisfaction. He revs up another, and nods. "It's old but I think it will run well. The fuel tank is almost full too."

"Should we go back in and get some food to take with us?" says Celeste.

"Too risky," says Adriana. "We can find food on the way."

Travis grimaces. "This thing is ugly," he says. "We should decorate it with some bright colors."

Adriana says, "We'll put you in charge of that as soon as we get to a safe place and find some paint."

Travis grins.

"Let's go everyone," says Adriana.

After opening the main garage door, Marcus takes the driver's seat. Adriana sits next to him, and Andy crawls up beside Adriana and lets out a couple of excited barks. The others choose places in the back. Vera slides the van's side door shut.

"Everybody ready?" says Adriana.

The van has a manual stick shift; Marcus presses down on the clutch and shoves it into first gear. When he lets up the clutch, the van shudders forward a few feet and then stalls. "Don't worry," he says. "I got this." His second try yields better results. He is able to get the van moving and even manages to slide into second.

They wind down a driveway and come to a three-way intersection.

Marcus points to the right. "That way must lead back to the city."

"I don't want to go back there," says Celeste.

"Neither do I," says Travis.

"I understand your reluctance," says Adriana, "but you heard what the visitors said. *They* united us. When I left here the first time, I sensed each of you and found you. Now that we're a family, I think we need to locate other families. Think of them as relatives. They're out there; I'm sure of it, although my directional sense isn't as specific as it was before. All I know is, to find them we need to go where there are lots of people."

"The city," says Travis.

"That's right," says Adriana. "And we shouldn't be frightened. We'll be fine. We have each other."

Marcus puts the van back into gear. As he releases the clutch, the thrill of anticipation infuses all seven of them.

All fourteen if you count the visitors.

Part Two: The Family Finds a Home

I

Adriana, Celeste, Travis, Marcus, and Sage are all sitting at the large dining table drinking tea, eating cookies, and watching the ocean when Vera comes down the spiral stairs.

It is early afternoon. The sky is clear, and light shines on the water.

"There's something you need to see," says Vera.

Everyone, including Andy, follows her upstairs.

Vera has added to the wall mural. "Don't get too close," she says. "It hasn't dried yet."

The new scene has the partially ruined city as background. Overlaying this is a configuration that resembles a mandala. At its center is a symbol consisting of seven gold points, one at the center and the other six surrounding it. Around this central symbol are six identical seven-pointed symbols in a concentric circle.

"The one in the middle," says Travis, pointing. "That's our family, isn't it?"

"I don't know," says Vera.

"I think it is," says Celeste. "But then what are the rest of these?"

"I don't know," says Vera. "It's like the other images: I came up and started painting by inspiration. I didn't have much of a plan in mind. Sometimes I figure it out afterwards and sometimes I don't."

"The rest are other families," says Adriana. "The ones we still have to find."

"But how can we do that?" says Marcus.

Andy can help! Andy can help!

Adriana smiles. "Come on, let's go back downstairs and finish our tea."

When they are all sitting with fresh full steaming cups before them, Sage says, "Won't we go out and look for them the same way you looked for us?"

"I didn't have to search, though," says Adriana. "I knew where to find you."

"Because of what they did to you," says Celeste.

"Maybe," says Adriana. "I've thought a lot about that. I don't think they gave me the ability to find you. I think they recognized that I had it already and sensitized me so that I could focus better. Their motivation was to destroy us, though. I think that in time families can find one another without their help."

"But how can *we* locate them?" says Travis. "Should we search the city?"

"The city is a big place," says Adriana. "And I don't think it will be easy to find other families if they don't realize they want to be found. I think this time we'll need a different approach. We may have to make ourselves visible so that they will come to us."

"What do you mean?" says Vera.

"We'll move to a bigger place that can hold more people, maybe somewhere inside the city. We'll slowly let people know who and what we are. That we've lost our memories. That we've come together as a family. Other confused people will seek us out. People who aren't interested will avoid us."

"Unless they feel threatened and attack," says Marcus.

"I don't think they will," says Adriana. "They're too disorganized, and I have the feeling that our visitors have means of defending themselves."

"People from that facility might attack," says Sage. "They will have more resources."

"We'll deal with them if they do," says Adriana.

*   *   *

Early the next morning Marcus, Sage, and Andy set out on foot towards the city. Their purpose is to scout out a new location to which the family can move.

In the meantime, Vera goes upstairs and continues painting. However, instead of continuing her vision into the future, she works on the other end of the mural that depicts the past. The images clarify for Adriana that when the visitors came they did not attack. The decimating war was fought only between various factions of humans, almost as if they had been waiting for an excuse to pulverize one another. In the aftermath of the conflict people tried to survive the best they could. A minority who had served as lifeboats for the visitors struggle to cope with lost memories and attempt reunification with the units to whom they belong.

Like her family.

It's an ongoing situation that's still in its early stages.

Travis too has been busying himself painting. The van is parked near a side of the house that is not visible from the road, and Travis is redecorating the exterior. From Vera he has obtained bright colors: purple, blue, green, red, orange, pink, and yellow. He is creating swirls, blotches, streaks, waves, spots, squiggles, and whatever else occurs to him. He focuses on the task for hours on end; when he enters the house to eat, drink, or use the bathroom his clothes are covered in paint stains but he is smiling. He keeps at it from early morning until sunset on the day that the scouting team leaves, stops to sleep, and then commences again from sunup until noon the following day.

He then calls Adriana, Celeste, and Vera to come see.

The van has become more than a vehicle of transportation. It is a screaming rainbow, a visual splendor, a bright beacon that is sure to attract attention wherever it goes.

"I have an idea," says Adriana. "We can use this. Vera, can you reproduce the mandala you painted upstairs on both sides of the van? Maybe with a dark background so that it's easily visible. If you don't mind that she covers a little of your work, Travis."

"No, I don't mind," says Travis. "That's all right."

"I'm thinking that it might serve as an advertisement," says Adriana. "Those who need to might recognize it."

Around noon the following day Marcus returns alone. After he calls the others together he says, "We found a place. It took us longer than expected because the large houses closer to town are all occupied. This one is set up on a hill overlooking the city and the harbor. It's got a great view. The house is huge: two floors and a basement and lots of rooms. The grounds are extensive, and a high wall surrounds the property. We think maybe it's still empty because you can't see it from the road. Also the interior is dirty and needs repairs."

"It sounds wonderful," says Adriana. "Are you sure it's not too remote?"

"It's only about an hour's walk from the center," says Marcus. "And like I said, anything closer was taken. We felt good about it. That's why Sage and Andy stayed there. They're waiting for us."

"We can at least go and see it," says Celeste.

"Of course we can," says Adriana. "Maybe we should walk there first, though, so we don't attract attention. We don't want anyone to know we're there yet. We want to get the place ready before we open it up to visitors."

II

They all eat a light meal together, and then Adriana, Celeste, Vera, and Travis follow Marcus along the winding coastal road to the city and through the rubble-strewn center. In scattered locations makeshift shops selling scavenged food, clothing, and other items have been opened. They also observe several construction sites similar to the one at which Marcus had been working. There are not many pedestrians. For the most part, the people who notice the family members pass regard them with befuddlement or suspicion.

As they begin their ascent of the two-lane road leading into the suburban hills, Adriana says, "Keep alert. Watch that we're not followed."

Once they leave what used to be the commercial area, though, and pass house after house surrounded by riotously overgrown lawns and gardens, they spot very few people. Occasionally a face regards them from a distant window; otherwise they are alone.

A dark cloud cover and brisk winds presage rain.

"Are we close?" says Celeste.

"Not much farther," says Marcus.

As the road continues into the hills, the houses become larger and more scattered.

Marcus says, "This way," and turns left onto an unpaved gravel driveway. They follow it through a stand of lush trees whose overhanging branches turn the already dark day into twilight. Abruptly they emerge before a metal gate set into a high solid-looking wall made of cinder blocks. The house is a few hundred meters away at the end of a concrete driveway that's partially blocked by overgrown foliage. Although it's of fairly modern design, the unkempt grounds and the chiaroscuro effect brought on by the approaching storm has given it a gothic ambiance.

"Wow," says Travis.

There is a loud screech when Marcus works the latch and another when he swings the gate open.

While Marcus closes the gate, Andy bounds down the driveway barking and wagging his tail. *Hello, hello! Welcome home, welcome home!*

Scattered raindrops begin to fall.

Everyone makes a run for the house.

Inside, Sage hugs Adriana, then Celeste, then Vera, then Travis, then Marcus, and then pats Andy on the head.

The hallway is dim and full of shadows.

"Is there electricity?" says Adriana.

"No, not yet," says Sage.

"I've checked the lines," says Marcus. "I think I can get it going again, but it will take time."

"Come on," says Sage. "I have a fire going in the living room, and there are plenty of candles."

The living room has a high ceiling with thick wood crossbeams, numerous couches and chairs, and a large stone fireplace framing warm glowing dancing flames.

"Oh, that's nice," says Travis.

"Yesterday Marcus and I explored this place thoroughly," says Sage. "The construction is sound. The interior is dirty, but there's very little mold or rot. There are six bedrooms, three bathrooms, a dining room, an enormous open basement area, and even a library, although it needs more books. Some food is stored in the pantry, and the wine cellar is fairly full."

"Wine cellar?" says Adriana.

"Yes," says Marcus.

"Well," says Adriana. "What does everyone think?"

"I don't care about the wine," says Vera.

"I don't mean that," says Adriana. "What do you think about the house? It looks like it needs a lot of work, but that's probably true of anyplace we find."

"Marcus and I like it," says Sage, "or we wouldn't have brought you here."

Raindrops begin to tap on the windows. Soon there is the steady drumming sound of a downpour.

"We're all here now," says Adriana. "Let's stay the night, look around in the morning, and then decide."

"I love the feeling of being safe and dry during rainfall," says Vera.

"I do too," says Celeste.

"The main stove is electric so it doesn't work yet," says Sage, "but I found an auxiliary one that uses gas. I cooked dinner: lentils in tomato sauce. I even managed to pan-fry some bread."

"I'm hungry," says Marcus.

"Let's bring it in here where it's warm," says Travis.

They load up bowls with lentil stew and set them on coffee tables in the living room. In the middle Sage sets hot sauce, salt, pepper, spoons, and a large platter full of flat bread. In the meantime, Marcus and Adriana go to the cellar and retrieve a few bottles of red wine.

Before they start in on the food and drink, they all click glasses. Sage says, "To family!"

For a time they eat silently. They don't converse until they have emptied their bowls, gone back for refills, and sat down again.

"Do you know what I wonder sometimes?" says Celeste. "I wonder if I had family before. Don't you all wonder that? We must have. Most of us anyway."

"I think about it, sure," says Vera.

Marcus nods.

Vera says, "From what I can gather, we lost our memories when the visitors arrived. There must be a correlation."

Marcus says, "They're in us, and yet they have never attempted to communicate with us."

"Yes they have," says Adriana, "One of them spoke to me at the clinic. And how else can you explain my ability to find all of you, and Andy's ability to communicate mind to mind with me, and Vera's ability to paint events before they happen?"

"Don't you wonder who we were before they arrived?" says Celeste.

"Of course I do," says Adriana. "And maybe someday we'll find out. Right now, though, it doesn't seem important compared to what we're doing now."

Sage says, "We think of the visitors being somehow like us, but what if they're not? What if they're way different?"

"They're obviously different," says Marcus. "None of us can jump out of our bodies into someone else."

"It's not just that," says Sage. "Vera's paintings picture them as arriving in vehicles like space ships, but that image could be figurative. What if they have no corporeality at all? What if the transport they used wasn't material?"

"What else could it be?" says Marcus.

"I don't know," says Sage. "Thought? Something we've never heard of?"

"Do you regret what's happened?" says Adriana. "Do you wish things were back the way they were before?"

"Of course not," says Sage. "Now I have a family. Behind me I have nothing. I'm just curious, that's all."

Adriana says, "I think a lot of people out there can't remember anything. They have nothing and they're all alone."

After a period of silence Vera says, "I'm tired."

"Me too," says Travis. "But I don't want to go into the upstairs darkness. I like it here."

Sage says, "This room, the kitchen, and the downstairs bathroom are the cleanest and warmest rooms in the house. If everyone wants, we can bring some mattresses and blankets in and sleep here tonight."

Everyone expresses approval of this plan.

Travis and Adriana commence clearing the tables and washing dishes. Sage, Marcus, Celeste, and Vera go after the bedding. Andy ducks out the kitchen dog door to relieve himself.

*   *   *

In the morning while Marcus starts working on the electricity, Sage gives Adriana, Celeste, Travis, and Vera a tour of the house. When she finishes leading them around the upstairs, main floor, and basement, she takes them outside, where they stroll on stone walkways through the overgrown grounds. The clouds have dissipated and the sky is clear and brilliantly blue. Although the gardens are unkempt, it is obvious that clearing the excess away will reveal an abundance of lovely, exotic, colorful plants.

Just as they reenter the house, the lights come on. A grinning Marcus joins them in the living room. "So what's next?" he says.

"That's it then?" says Adriana. "Is everyone happy with this place?"

"Why not?" says Vera.

"It's going to take a lot of work to clean and fix it," says Adriana, "but we don't need to do it all right away. I'm sure that others will come, and when they do, they can help us. In the meantime, the first thing we need to do is prepare some bedrooms. There's plenty of space for everyone."

"But I don't want to stay alone by myself," says Celeste.

"Neither do I," says Travis.

"Or me," says Sage.

It turns out that nobody wants their own room, so they decide to pair up: Vera and Sage in one room, Marcus and Travis in another, and Adrian, Celeste, and Andy in a third.

"That will save plenty of space for newcomers," says Adriana.

They all go upstairs to choose rooms. They then spend the rest of the morning dusting, sweeping, washing bedding, and making beds. They find clothing in the various closets and redistribute it according to sizes, tastes, and predilections.

Back downstairs, they confer again.

"Shouldn't we bring the van here?" says Marcus.

"I need my paints too," says Vera.

"We could use the food that's in the old house," says Sage.

"The van is very bright," says Vera. "It will attract attention. Should we go at night?"

"Why?" says Adriana. "We're here to attract attention. We don't have to hide. Imagine you are out in the city somewhere by yourself, like you were before, lonely, having forgotten who you are. Seeing the van might ignite something inside that leads you to your family. Wouldn't you want it to happen sooner rather than later?"

"Yes," says Vera.

"If you're up to it, why not go now?" says Adriana. "Load the van, and drive back while there's still light."

"I'm fine to go now," says Marcus.

Vera nods.

"Can I go too?" says Travis.

"Sure," says Marcus. "Why not?"

"How about you, Andy?" says Adriana. "Do you want to go or stay?"

I want to stay and explore the garden!

Adriana chuckles. "All right, then, go ahead."

Andy barks once, wags his tail, runs to the kitchen, and scurries out the dog door.

III

Harrison finally decides to leave his isolated little cabin. It's set in the midst of a forest of tall evergreens, and nearby a creek trickles gently over a bed of smooth stones. He has been content enough here for an indeterminate amount of time, but now he realizes that it is time to move on. For one thing, the food is getting low. For another, he has a vague indefinable feeling that he needs to be somewhere else. A sense of unease that he cannot define has gripped him. He can't remember how he got to where he is or what he used to do before he became a cabin dweller. He has searched for clues throughout his small home but has found nothing that might tell him about his past life. His hair and beard are white; his hands are mottled; his joints ache first thing in the morning. These things tell him that he used to be younger than he is now. He chuckles at how absurd and pointless a conclusion he has come to.

In a small backpack he places a change of clothes, a toiletry kit, a book, a blanket, a bottle of water, and enough food for a day. He realizes that in traveling so light he will be dependent on what he finds along the way, but he has no choice. He knows through hikes he has taken in the woods that he cannot carry much or he'll soon get a relentless ache in his lower back.

The pack sits ready on the kitchen table. He hoists it onto his back, steps out onto the small porch, and closes the cabin door behind him. This cabin has been his safe place, his refuge, and his sanctuary. When darkness and inclement weather frightened him, closing himself into it gave him a sense of security. Now he is leaving the protection of the four walls and is striking out for... Where? He has no idea where he is going.

However, once he turns his back on his former domicile and starts down the rutted track, his disquiet vanishes. A feeling of peace, calm, and equanimity pervades him. His senses reach out to embrace his surroundings. He smells evergreen sap and the mulch on the forest floor; he hears the crunch of his footsteps on the path and the songs of birds overhead; he feels the gentle soothing coolness in the shadows of the trees. There is something right about this walk. He does not approach it aimlessly as he has his jaunts through the woods. This time he is going somewhere. This time he has a destination, even though he doesn't know what that destination is.

He measures time in abstractions because he doesn't have a watch. After awhile, he comes to a paved road with staggered lines in the middle marking the difference between two lanes. To the right, the road goes uphill and disappears around a curve. To the left, the road goes downhill and disappears around a curve.

The choice for Harrison is simple. He will go left because he is already tired. He can't imagine trudging uphill for long; downhill will be easier.

As soon as he starts downhill he receives the conviction that he has made the correct choice. However, that doesn't make the walk any easier. Within a short time his legs ache and his head throbs. He goes as long as he can, dizziness and unease increasing, until he stops to rest on a boulder by the roadside. He continues in this way, walking and halting, walking and halting, slowly making his way towards...whatever. During one of his rests he looks back in longing at the way that he has come and sighs. He realizes that if he had the strength he would walk back up the hill to his cabin and abandon his quest. He also realizes that would be the end of him because he would never again have the courage to leave. Just as well, then, that he has committed before he realized what he was really in for.

Around midmorning he stops to drink some water and eat a homemade roll and a few pieces of dried fruit. He has been considering hitchhiking, but until now no vehicles have passed by and he has seen no other people. Occasionally he notices paths leading off into the forest, indicative perhaps of other cabin dwellers, but he is not about to expend what little strength he has in going to investigate. His way lies along the road, at least for now, but he's not sure how much longer he will have the energy to pursue it.

His mood has approached dangerously close to despair when he catches his first glimpse of the sea and the city that lies beside it. The sight doesn't assuage his weariness, but it gives him fresh hope that if he perseveres he can make it that far.

Still, he walks more slowly now. He is actually trudging instead of walking. He knows he has done the right thing but sometimes knowledge of rightness is not enough. He supposes that many people fail to reach their goals; it may be that more people fail than succeed, in fact, and it would not be surprising at all if he turns out to be one of the failures. Before giving up, though, he decides to walk just a little longer. After all, he has come far. He has started to pass scattered houses in the city's outlying suburbs. By this time it is late afternoon. The houses appear to be empty, but he can always stop and sleep in one of them if he is too exhausted to continue.

Just a little farther.

He doesn't know what is compelling him to go on or where the reserves of energy are coming from. He is gripped by an eagerness that he cannot explain.

And then abruptly he pauses before an unpaved gravel driveway that heads off into a stand of trees to his right. No house is visible; the residence must lie beyond the dense foliage. He hears the faint clamor of music, but that's not what has caused him to stop. His movement has been arrested because he realizes that *this is his path*. This is the direction that he must take; there is no doubt about it.

Onward, then, with gravel crunching underfoot. Through the trees until he arrives at a metal gate set in a high cinder wall.

The gate is slightly ajar.

Beyond is an immense two-story mansion. Numerous people are engaged in various activities around the spacious grounds.

What is this place?

Harrison slips through the gap in the gate and then hesitates, concerned that someone might accuse him of trespassing.

A few meters away to his right a slim young man of about ten or twelve is engaged in painting the inside surface of the cinder wall. A thick coat of white has already been laid down, and on it he is adding bright abstract patterns of colors such as red, orange, green, blue, and yellow with narrow bordering tracks of white or black. Triangles, rectangles, pentagons, hexagons, circles, and other geometric shapes are surrounded by loops and swirls and waves and shimmers. Harrison can make no sense of it, but then again, maybe he's not supposed to be able to. The design has its own stark chaotic coherence and beauty.

As Harrison approaches, the boy looks up from contemplating his artwork and smiles. "Hi," he says. "Welcome. My name is Travis."

"I'm Harrison."

"You are for now at least."

"What do you mean by that?"

"Oh, nothing. This place has a way of changing people."

"That's some eye-catching painting you've done."

"Thanks. I like for things to be colorful and interesting."

"Does it mean anything?"

"Not intentionally, but you never know, right?"

"I suppose so."

"If you like more realistic illustrations, you should go look at Vera's work. She's over there at the other end of the compound." Travis points with a paint-spattered finger.

"Thanks. Uh, Travis, if you don't mind my asking, what is this place?"

Travis smiles even more broadly than before. "Why, this is home, Mister Harrison. This is home."

Harrison nods and wanders off vaguely in the direction that Travis has indicated. He follows a pathway that meanders towards the house. As he approaches, he notices where the music has been coming from. A low wooden platform has been constructed beside the main entrance to the house, and people are setting up guitars, flutes, a keyboard, drums, amplifiers, and microphones. In the process of testing the equipment, musicians burst spontaneously into melodious tunes.

The path winds around the outside of the house. At various spots in the garden, people are intently tending plants: pruning, watering, and pulling weeds.

Near the back entrance, which leads into the kitchen, a table is set up. It is loaded with rolls, bagels, croissants, salads, slices of fresh fruit, and other food items.

A woman carries out a large steaming pot of stew and sets it on a hot pad. "Hello," she says. "I'm Sage. I don't remember seeing you around. Are you new here?"

"Uh, yes. I just arrived. My name is Harrison."

"Are you hungry, Harrison? Grab a plate and help yourself to anything you like. We haven't set up the tables and chairs out here yet, but you can sit at the dining table inside while you eat."

Harrison abruptly realizes that he is famished. His stomach feels hollow and so much saliva fills his mouth when he looks at the food that he has to wipe his face with his sleeve. "Well, maybe just a little if you don't mind."

"Harrison, it's yours. Take as much as you want. Fill up a plate. Here's a bowl for the stew."

He eagerly complies.

"All right for now? Follow me," says Sage. She leads him through the kitchen and sits him down at the table. "We have beer, wine, and water. Which would you like?"

"Water would be fine, thank you."

Sage brings a glass full of water and then says, "If there's anything else you need, please let me know. I'm going to continue preparing for supper." She then goes off without waiting for a reply.

For a time Harrison sits at the table alone attending to the food. He eats steadily until he has finished everything except a last morsel of roll with which he wipes the inside of the stew bowl. So intent has he been on his meal that he hasn't noticed a woman approach from the interior of the house. He looks up when she sits down opposite him.

"I'm sorry," she says. "Did I interrupt?"

"No, I'm done," he says as he finishes chewing the last mouthful.

"Would you like some more?"

"No, thank you."

"I'm Adriana." She reaches across and shakes Harrison's hand.

"I'm Harrison. Why is everyone here so hospitable?"

"So far everyone who's showed up has been family."

"Family? How is that possible? The people I've seen don't look anything alike."

"You're the oldest so far," says Adriana. "I hope you don't mind my saying so."

"No, I don't mind. But..."

"You said your name was Harrison? Where have you come from?"

"I was living alone in a cabin in the hills."

"And before that?"

"I don't remember."

"Don't let it bother you. None of us can remember much."

"Why?"

"Something happened. I'll explain later. So what made you decide to leave your cabin?"

"I don't know. It wasn't easy; I felt secure there. I got the urge that I needed to be somewhere else."

"That's right. You needed to be here."

"Why?"

"Because here you're with family."

"You said that earlier. What does it mean?"

"Not exactly what it used to mean. Take your time. Wander around. Get to know people. Consider this your home. We'll find you a place to sleep later. There are bathrooms upstairs and downstairs in case you need them. We're having a sort of informal event tonight."

"What's the occasion?"

"Nothing special. It's just for fun. Oh, by the way, if you don't mind, I think you have another name."

"Oh? What is it?"

"Walker."

"Walker? Why Walker?"

"I don't know. But I suppose you walked here, didn't you?"

"Didn't everyone?"

Adriana smiles.

"Travis told me to expect changes," says Walker. "I met him at the gate."

"He's got a lot of curiosity and sense of wonder," says Adriana. "Do you know where we found him? He was trapped in an underground tunnel where someone had sent him to recover supplies. They'd left him there in the darkness to die."

At this point, Andy runs in, tail wagging, and licks Walker's hand. Walker strokes Andy's head and Andy's tail wags faster.

"Andy here rescued Travis," says Adriana. "He dug him out. Andy, this is Walker."

Walker, Walker! My family! Welcome!

"Andy welcomes you to the family."

"You can understand him?"

"*I* can. Just me. You know, Walker, I've got a feeling about you. Within the larger family, clusters form. My cluster is made up of seven members. You've already met some of them: Travis, Sage, and Andy."

"Andy is a family member?"

Family! Andy is family!

"Yes. In each cluster there seems to be a head of household; not a boss who tells people what to do, but someone who is responsible for gathering everyone together and keeping them together. I think you may be a head of household."

"Me? How can that be? I can barely take care of myself."

"I don't know. Like I said, I just have a feeling. If it's true, people may come to you, or you may have to go out and find them. Maybe Vera can tell you more. Why don't you go see her? She's over there by the wall."

"Travis mentioned her."

"Yes, they're both artists. But Vera does more than create art. Go and find out. Or rest and go later. It's up to you."

"I suppose I'm rested and fueled enough. Nice to meet you, Adriana."

"Nice to meet you too, Walker."

Adriana smiles and then leaves.

Walker takes his dishes to the kitchen and then meanders out into the garden.

Kneeling on the ground in front of the wall opposite the gate is a woman holding a palette and a thin brush. More painting supplies are on a nearby table. Unlike Travis's flamboyant abstractions, this woman's work is meticulously rendered. It consists of a collage of scenes that appears to tell a story.

"Are you Vera?"

The woman turns, stands, and smiles. Like all the smiles that Walker has received so far here, this one is simple and sincere and he can tangibly feel its warmth. "Yes, I am."

"I'm Walker. Your work is impressive."

"Thank you. Over there I've reproduced some scenes I painted at our last location. These are more recent."

Walker scans the images. He squints and looks more closely. "Why, that looks like me as I hiked down the hill today. But that's impossible."

"Why?"

"Because I just got here. How could you have known?"

"I don't know. When I'm painting, the rules of time don't seem to work the same way. It's happened before."

"What's that symbol?"

"It's a cluster."

"Adriana mentioned clusters."

"Yes, they're smaller units within the larger family."

"Adriana said that too. Why is that cluster near me?"

"I don't know. I'm sure you'll find out eventually."

IV

She knows it isn't her real name; she chose it just recently from a volume on the bookshelf. Lena. She can't decide if it suits her or not because she's not sure what her personality used to be like. Right now and for the past several days or weeks she has been mainly perplexed and frightened. She remembers hearing gunshots and explosions, feeling the floor shake, watching concrete dust sift down from the ceiling, curling up in terror on the single bed in the corner, protecting the swaddled baby with her curved body.

That's another thing: the baby. She supposes that he must be hers because her breasts are full of milk and he nurses vigorously whenever she gives him the opportunity. However, she cannot remember having him, how old he is, or even his name. She has given him one at random too: Ben. He is a profoundly stoic child. Most of the time when he is awake he quietly watches her. He never cries. Often he kicks his legs and waves his arms as any baby would, but Lena gets the impression that these actions are deliberate; he is methodically exercising his limbs to strengthen them.

How can that be? That's not how babies are supposed to behave, is it? She also finds it puzzling that Ben does not communicate his needs by making noise. Instead, he looks at her with disconcerting intensity and she knows whether he is hungry, tired, or wants to be placed upon the bright blue plastic potty. There are diapers stored in the basement, but Ben distains them. Lena remembers changing him only once, back when the explosions and gunfire were happening, and after that it has been clear that diapers are unnecessary. Is that normal? She can't remember.

She can't recall how she got to this place either. It's a basement storage room with narrow windows on two sides, although all but one of the windows has been blocked with black construction paper. She has a bed for herself and a crib for the baby, a few changes of clothes, and plenty of disposable diapers. A faucet over a sink dispenses water that is apparently clean. A fridge and some cupboards contain food that once seemed to be plenteous but now has almost all run out.

The thought of ascending the steps and venturing into the outer world in search of supplies fills Lena with terror. She has no choice, though; it's move or starve.

She puts on a cloth baby sling, cinches the straps, and lifts the watchful baby into position against her chest. He's heavy and his weight is unwieldy; her lower back begins to ache almost immediately. In his wordless yet precise way he offers her suggestions on how she can adjust the sling so he can ride more easily.

Lena hasn't packed anything to take with her. She sees this initial venture topside as a reconnoitering mission. In fact, she is hoping that she'll find some food on an upper floor of the same building, take it back downstairs, and seal up the door again. She is sure that she will be unable to feel safe when exposed to whatever is outside.

She ascends the stairs slowly and pauses at the top to listen. When she is sure that she hears nothing, she pulls the deadbolt, turns the latch, and opens the door.

She's in a kitchen that smells strongly of mold and faintly of decaying food. The cupboards are open and appear to have been ransacked.

Silence. And then, the sound of a scrape and then a thump from just around the corner.

Lena wants to turn around and lock herself and the baby back in the basement, but to what end? Instead, she hurries to the hallway and says, "Who's there?"

The next sound is light footsteps running up stairs.

Lena follows. As she reaches the upstairs, she sees a door close down the hall.

She hesitates. She doesn't want to frighten anyone and she certainly doesn't want to endanger herself or the baby. Still, she wants to know who has been living here right above her hideaway. She slowly turns the knob and pushes the door open.

Two children stare at her from near an open window. One is a boy who appears to be about four or five, and the other is a girl of about seven. They seem to be getting ready to crawl over the window sill out onto the roof.

"Wait," says Lena. "Don't be afraid. I won't hurt you. Who are you?"

It is clear from their expressions that they don't know any more about their pasts than Lena does about hers.

"Do you have names? I'm Lena."

The children don't answer.

Baby Ben nudges Lena mentally and projects a thought into her consciousness, a thought that she immediately realizes is true.

"I'm your mother," says Lena. "I don't know if I was before but I am now. I'm going to take care of you."

The children remain still and silent, but their apprehensiveness seems to have subsided.

"I couldn't remember my name either," says Lena. "I had to make one up. I'm going to give you names too so it's easier to talk together. You can change them later if you like." She points to the boy. "You can be Steve." And then to the slightly older girl. "And you can be Edith. This baby, your brother, is named Ben. All right? Now... Are you hungry?"

The children look at each other, and then Edith nods.

"Let's go downstairs and see if there is anything to eat."

In the kitchen Lena finds a dusty highchair. She cleans it off and places Ben inside, where he sits quietly watching and listening.

Steve and Edith sit at the table while Lena searches the fridge, drawers, and cupboards. Everything fresh and in plastic or cardboard packages has been opened, edibles have been consumed, and the bin overflows with rubbish. On the shelves, though, Lena finds a large quantity of untouched canned food.

She sets some on the counter. "Have you two been here a long time?" she says.

Edith nods.

"As long as you can remember?"

She nods again.

"Why didn't you eat these? Wait... You don't know how to open them, do you?"

Edith shakes her head.

"Can you talk?"

"Yes," says Edith.

Steve turns to Edith in surprise.

"It's all right," says Edith to Steve. "I think she's safe." To Lena she says, "We decided not to talk to anyone unless we trusted them."

"Have you met anyone else?"

"No."

"Have you left the house?"

"No."

Lena smiles. "Well, first things first." She pulls a can opener out of a drawer. "What would you like to eat? There are beans, ravioli, vegetables, and other things. Look, you can see by the pictures."

After they make their selections, Lena chooses something too, and then they eat out of the cans with spoons. Edith and Steve both ask for more.

When they are all finished, Lena puts the dirty cans and utensils in the sink before picking up Ben and nursing him. When he's finished eating, he nods off to sleep. Lena carries him upstairs and places him on a bed as Steve and Edith trail behind. Half-shutting the bedroom door, Lena says, "You two look like you could use a bath. Have you been washing up regularly?"

Edith shakes her head.

"I thought not. Do you have some other clothes you can change into?"

"No," says Edith.

"Never mind. I'll wrap you in towels while I wash your clothes. Who wants to go first?"

Lena discovers that the hot water works, so she washes out the bathtub and fills it with warm water. When Steve enters the water he sits placidly as if he doesn't know what to do next. Lena scrubs him down, empties out the water, and rinses him under the shower. She repeats the procedure with Edith.

Lena then finds toothbrushes and toothpaste. Thinking that the children might not remember what to do, she demonstrates. They pick up on it right away, though, causing Lena to suppose that they, and by inference she, must have inherent recollections of habitual activities.

The shades and curtains in the house are all drawn shut, but Lena can tell from the fading light coming through the cracks that it is late. She washes the children's clothes in the bathtub and then hangs them on the shower rod. She takes Steve and Edith to the bedroom where she first found them and puts them to bed, and then she partially disrobes and goes to lie down beside Ben, pulling the sheet and blanket up over them. Within minutes she hears soft footsteps. Without a sound Edith and Steve slip under the covers, one on each side of Lena and the baby.

The four of them sleep through the night without incident. In the morning Lena feels so ebullient and fearless that she draws back the curtains and lifts the shades on the upstairs windows. Sunlight pours in. The brilliant blue sky is clear of clouds. The house sits on a slight slope in a residential area that appears strangely deserted. Down the hill and beyond a partially devastated commercial area pocked with several construction sites is the harbor.

Lena takes her time feeding the children and cleaning up afterwards. She wants to go slow and savor the experience of getting to know her new larger family. If in fact it is new. Were these her children before? They don't look much like one another, but of course they could have been fathered by different men. She comes to the conclusion that the situation as it was before doesn't matter. With each passing moment she becomes more convinced that as of now and into the future these are her children and this is her family.

However, there is something about baby Ben that Lena finds disconcerting. He doesn't behave like a baby at all, at least in his mind. How does Lena know this? Because he is continually passing on to her thoughts, impressions, observations, and suggestions. By midday he seems to have become impatient with Lena's lassitude. After a quick nap, he makes it clear to her that they can't stay where they are. They are needed elsewhere.

"Needed?" says Lena. "By whom?"

Steve and Edith have been sitting at the table drawing with colored pencils. They look up, startled at the outburst, obviously wondering who their mother just spoke to.

Ben doesn't answer in words. He creates an awareness of the tiny glowing family bond that the four of them have begun to create and nurture, and then his thoughts go out to the edge of the city, not far from where they are, to a place where instead of the tiny flame they have kindled there is a raging conflagration of togetherness and unity. Lena is overwhelmed by the intensity of it, not because it frightens her but because it is so profound and sublime. She feels inexorably drawn to it. They will be safe there. They will belong.

"Children," she says, "would you like to take a walk?"

Steve and Edith look at each other.

"A walk?" says Edith.

"We don't have to if you're too tired," says Lena, despite Ben's somber mental insistence.

"I'm not tired," says Steve.

"I'm not either," says Edith. "It's just that we haven't been outside since... Since... I can't remember."

"Then it will be fun, won't it?" says Lena. "It will be an adventure."

"An adventure?" says Steve. His expression brightens.

"Should we bring anything?" says Edith.

Lena considers their ephemeral destination. "I don't think so," she says. "It's not far. Use the bathroom, drink some water, and then we'll be on our way."

One of Lena's discoveries while exploring the house has been a stroller. When they are all ready, she places silent, attentive Ben in the seat and straps him in. She's grateful that she won't have to carry him in the sling.

They follow a street that takes them to the decimated central part of town, which they have to skirt before getting to another road that will take them into the hills. The sidewalks and streets are cracked and pitted. They move slowly, and sometimes Lena needs to lift the stroller over obstructions. One street is completely blocked with wreckage from ruined buildings and they have to circumnavigate the area by taking a detour of several blocks. The four of them are uneasy and silent as they wend their way past the remains of shops and offices with glassless windows and doorless frames leading off into vague eerie darkness.

When they come to a broader road that is relatively free of rubbish, Ben indicates that this is the way they must take.

"Look, here's our road," says Lena. "This looks easier, doesn't it?"

Before one of the children can answer, a voice behind them says, "Not so fast, lady. What's the rush?"

Three men with filthy clothes and filthier faces saunter out of the narrow alley the family has just traversed.

"Hello," says Lena. "You're the first people we've seen. Where have you come from?"

One of the men says, "We were working nearby and we saw you pass."

"Well, it was nice to meet you," says Lena, "but we need to be on our way."

"Like I said, not so fast. We have a quick business transaction in mind."

"I'm sorry. We don't have time."

"Maybe you can make time."

As the one man speaks, the other two circle around until Lena and the children are surrounded.

"Please leave us alone," says Lena.

"We're not going to hurt you. We'll even pay you. It will only take a little time and then you can be on your way."

"It's not possible," says Lena. "I have children with me."

"They'll be fine as long as you cooperate."

"You know, that girl looks just about old enough to be hired out as a tunnel crawler."

The men look Edith over thoughtfully.

"No, she's a little too small and scrawny. They like them older and stronger so they can haul more goods. Although..."

Lena keeps one hand on the stroller and with the other encircles Steve and Edith.

"Look, we'll make a deal with you, lady. We won't take your kids if you do as we say. Last chance before we force the issue."

One of the men looks dubious. "I don't know about this. Are you sure? We can get plenty down by the waterfront."

"Yeah, but we have to pay for it. This one, I've decided, will be for free. That's the price for us to leave her kids alone."

"Please, no," says Lena.

And then from farther down the road Lena hears an unusual sound. At first she can't identify it, but then she realizes that it's a vehicle. She and the children have seen a few cars in passing but they have all been unused for a long time. Some are covered in dust and debris, some are crushed by fallen sections of buildings, and most have their windows smashed out.

The vehicle rounds a corner and comes into sight. It's no ordinary car, though; it's a large van that is flamboyantly festooned with all the colors of the rainbow. It is so incongruous in this decimated setting that Lena has to blink and look again to be sure that it is truly there. Three people, a man, a woman, and a boy, sit inside on the front seat. They are all smiling, obviously enjoying themselves.

Lena gasps. There's something about these people...

Ben confirms her suspicions.

The driver stops the van and all three of them get out. Ignoring the three men, the driver says to Lena, "You look like you're heading up the hill. We'd be happy to give you a lift. My name is Marcus. This is Vera, and that's Travis."

"Now just a minute," says the man who has been doing most of the talking. "You're intruding here where you don't belong. Get back in that thing and keep moving."

Marcus is still smiling. "You're out of your league here, and I suggest you quit while you're uninjured. This family is under our protection, and we'll do anything to keep them safe. Anything. At the same time, we don't want to hurt anyone. Are you sure you want to risk this?"

The spokesman looks as if he wants to make an issue of it, but the other two are mumbling and backing down.

Marcus says, "Would you and your children like a ride, ma'am?"

Lena is too overcome with relief to speak, so she nods.

Travis takes Steve and Edith's hands and says, "Come on. We can sit in the back. It's a lot of fun."

The children grin and go with him.

Lena picks up Ben, who is radiating contentment.

"We can put that stroller in the back too," says Vera. "You can sit in front with us if you like. The ride's not long. Have you by any chance been looking for us?"

"I don't know," says Lena. "I think so. Ben says so."

"Who is Ben?" says Vera. "The boy?"

"No," says Lena. "The baby. Does that sound strange?"

"It doesn't," says Vera. "Maybe before, but not now. A lot has changed, hasn't it?"

Lena smiles. She, Ben, and Vera climb onto the front passenger seats.

Marcus is about to slide the side door of the van shut when one of the men that accosted Lena and the children sidles up. The other two have disappeared back into the shattered streets. "Excuse me," he says.

Marcus, still gripping the door handle, pauses.

"My name is Smith, I think. At least someone called me that. I followed those men because, well, I'm confused. The truth is... I don't know what's happening. I've been working for my needs during the day and getting drunk at night, but I can't remember what I used to do before this. I know this might sound straightforward, and you have no reason to trust me, but if it's possible I'd like to come with you too."

"We're all confused," says Marcus, "but it's starting to clear up as we go along. Come on, then."

V

Louisa knocks twice and then enters the supervisor's office. The space inside is already crowded with half a dozen attendants, the supervisor, and three heavy armed men that Louisa doesn't recognize who are clad in makeshift khaki uniforms.

"All right," says the supervisor. "We're all here. We have an update on the escapees. Officer?"

"We've found them," says one of the men in uniform. "It wasn't difficult. They haven't been trying to hide. In fact, they painted the van they stole in bright colors and have been driving it around the city as if it's an advertisement. They're squatting in a large abandoned residence just outside of town. Other suspected carriers are staying with them."

"These people are contaminated," says the supervisor. "As long as they are at large they put the rest of the population at risk. We've got to either bring them back here for purging or eliminate them."

"What do you mean by eliminate them?" asks Louisa.

"Shoot to kill, ma'am," says a uniformed officer.

Louisa wants to object, but she sees that the others are all tight-jawed, determined, and ready for action. She wonders if it will be wise for her to venture an opposing opinion in the heat of the moment. Instead, she remains mum and listens.

The supervisor says, "The militia are short staffed right now; this isn't the only insurrection. They can't send any more help. That's why they're deputizing all of you. They are going to issue weapons to you, and we are going to ride with these men. We are going to do our part to cleanse humanity and bring things back to normal. Do you understand?"

After a chorus of "yes ma'am," the supervisor says, "Let's go."

"Right now?" says Louisa.

"We can't afford to wait," says the supervisor. "What if they relocate? No, we've got to hit them now and hit them hard. I hope they cooperate, but if not..." She leaves the sentence unfinished.

The uniformed men issue pistols and holsters to the attendants. They take them around the side of the building to an open field and show them how to hold the weapon, release the safety, and pull the trigger. Each attendant has a chance to fire off a few rounds for practice. The gun feels awkward and unwieldy in Louisa's hand. She hopes fervently that she doesn't have to use it. She's grateful when practice is over and she shoves the weapon back into its holster.

"The safety," says her instructor.

"What?"

"The safety. You forgot to engage it. Do you want to accidentally shoot off your foot?"

"Oh, yes. Thank you. Do you really think we'll be at all effective with only a few minutes of practice? I would think we'd be in the way. We might even endanger you."

The instructor smiles grimly. "The key, ma'am, is to shoot from close range. Get the end of that barrel right up to their chest or the side of their head and then fire. That way you'll have no trouble taking them out."

"But I don't know if I can..."

At this point the supervisor walks up. "Is there a problem?"

The instructor says, "This one is having qualms about our mission."

The supervisor turns to Louisa and raises an eyebrow.

Louisa says, "How can we just go in there and kill them? There must be another way. They're still people."

"Are they?" says the supervisor. "They would be if we could get them here and help them, but we've already seen where attempting to do that has got us. Don't worry; we'll give them another chance. If they don't take it, though, we have no option but to eradicate the threat."

The supervisor assembles the armed attendants outside the garage. Inside, the three members of the militia are behind the wheels of the three blue vans. The engines are already running.

"We're bringing all three vehicles so we'll have room in case anyone wants to come back with us," says the supervisor. "I know this goes far beyond what we usually expect of you, but in a state of emergency we all have to rise up to the needs of the moment. Still, if anyone feels they cannot handle this situation, tell me now and you can wait here."

Louisa wants to scream, "Me! I can't handle it. I think all of you are crazy. We can't simply kill people because we don't understand them." She's not sure exactly why she remains silent. She's ambivalent and confused; that's part of it. She doesn't know what she'll do if she has to stay back here all by herself wondering if things have gone smoothly or they haven't and a bloodbath is taking place. She feels a sense of inevitability about it all, as if she is in a small boat without oars or rudder in the midst of a swift-flowing river.

She rides in a van with the supervisor, the man who instructed her in the use of her pistol, and a male attendant who seems eager for action. They drive along small winding roads through the hills, catching occasional glimpses of the city and harbor below. Louisa can't remember ever having been on these roads before. The city itself seems vaguely unfamiliar, as if she recalls it only from an old photograph.

After driving for about half an hour or so, the vans park in a line along the side of the road. The entire company hikes down a driveway, past an obviously deserted house, and through an overgrown garden to a fence at the edge of a terrace.

"There they are," says one of the militia.

About five hundred yards down the slope is a spacious compound surrounded by a high cinder brick wall. The house is immense. Scattered throughout the garden are individuals and groups of people engaged in various activities such as strolling, gardening, and painting the sides of the walls.

"Good," says the supervisor. "Is there any way we can know that they're all there?"

"No," says the militiaman. "We don't have the personnel for long-term observation. But from what we've been able to ascertain, most of them stay here; only a few go out periodically for supplies. When they do, they use the stolen van. It's currently parked inside the garage."

"All right," says the supervisor. "The first step is to give them an invitation and a warning."

"If we do that they may try to run," says the militiaman. "Some might escape. Shouldn't we go in, take them by surprise, and capture them all at once?"

"They'll have a better chance of responding well to treatment if they submit to it voluntarily," says the supervisor. "We have to give them a chance."

The militiaman nods towards one of his colleagues. "He's had sniper training. He'll be able to pick them off if they try to scale the walls. Agreed?"

"Yes."

"So how are you going to deliver your message?"

"Someone will have to go down to them."

"Not one of us," says the militiaman. "We've got to remain in position."

"No," says the supervisor. "One of them."

She turns to the attendants, who are huddled together near the fence. "We need a volunteer to take a message to the suspects."

The attendants do not exactly take a step backwards, but their expressions clearly indicate their trepidation. One says, "What if whatever is wrong with them is contagious?"

"It's not," says the supervisor. "You know this. You've been around them before."

Another says, "What if they attack us?"

"They're not going to do that," says the supervisor.

"How do you know? They killed one of us, and they threatened to kill you."

"I think that death was an accident," says the supervisor. "And they didn't hurt me."

"But they could have," says an attendant.

After a long silence, Louisa says, "I'll go." She's not exactly sure why she is volunteering. She is frightened, but at the same time she feels strangely drawn to the people she sees below in the garden.

The supervisor contemplates Louisa for a moment and then says, "Good. Thank you. You're a brave woman. Listen carefully. Here's what I want you to say..."

After the supervisor has briefed Louisa, one of the militiamen drives her down the road to the track leading to the mansion.

As Louisa walks beneath the stand of trees and comes to the metal gate in the cinder block wall, she has second thoughts. What is she doing here? Why did she volunteer? She has the urge to turn around and run the other way. Instead, she slowly advances and steps through the open gate, her mouth dry, her heart pounding.

To her right is a paint-splashed boy painting colors onto the inside of the wall. "Hello," he says. "I'm Travis. What's your name?"

"I'm... My name is Louisa."

Travis smiles. "Welcome, Louisa. How did you find us?"

"I... Uh... I have to speak to someone in charge."

"In charge?"

"A leader. Who is the leader?"

Travis ruminates. "It's not like that. We don't really have leaders. We're a family."

"A family?"

"Maybe you should talk to Adriana. She can explain it better than I can. Go inside the main entrance to the house and ask anyone where Adriana is."

"Should I just walk right in?"

"Of course. Why not? I'll see you later, Louisa. If your name is still Louisa when we meet next."

"What do you mean by that?"

"You'll find out."

Louisa walks slowly towards the house. To her left beyond a low hedge, two young children play with a ball on a patch of lawn while a woman sits on a bench nearby nursing a baby. The baby abruptly raises his head and looks at Louisa with a somber expression and then goes back to his suckling. To her right, a man is pulling weeds at the edge of a bush full of luxuriant yellow roses. He notices Louisa, smiles, and waves.

She briefly glances up the hill towards where the supervisor, the attendants, and the militia are waiting. She doesn't spot them.

The front door of the mansion is ajar. Louisa considers knocking but she gets the feeling that it would be ludicrous to do so. Instead, she pushes the door open wider and steps in.

From the hallway she enters the spacious living room, where a woman and an older man sit on a couch near the unlit fireplace.

Louisa immediately recognizes Adriana from her last visit to the facility.

Adriana raises her head and says, "I know you. You're one of the attendants that we locked in the cafeteria when we escaped. Are you all right?"

"I... I'm fine."

"Why didn't you come with us then?"

"Come with you?"

"Of course. And yet here you are now so all is well."

"What do you mean?"

"Didn't you come to join our family?"

With a rush of recognition Louisa realizes that is exactly why she has come. However, confusion overwhelms her so she says, "Actually, I'm here to deliver a message."

"What's your name?"

"Louisa."

"Are you sure?"

"I..."

"How did you come by that name?"

"It was on some paperwork."

"Yours?"

"I think so."

"But you don't remember if it's your real name, do you?"

Louisa shakes her head.

"Come and relax, Louisa."

She sits on a couch opposite Adriana and the old man.

"This is Walker," says Adriana.

Walker nods and smiles.

"I think that Walker might know what your name is."

Louisa looks at him expectantly.

"I suppose I'm not as good at this as Adriana," says Walker. Louisa is a fine name. You can keep it if you like."

"I haven't really thought about it," says Louisa. "I didn't know I had a choice."

"Around here you can change it every day if you want," says Walker, "although it might get a bit confusing if you do."

Adriana says, "Louisa, you mentioned a message. Who is it from?"

"The supervisor."

"Ah." Adriana turns to Walker and says, "I told you about the facility. The supervisor is the one in charge. The one I threatened. So they've found us. Took them long enough." To Louisa she says, "What did she say?"

Louisa passes on the supervisor's warning and explains about the armed militiamen and attendants waiting on the hillside.

"Do you think we should call the others indoors as a precaution?" says Adriana.

"It wouldn't hurt," says Walker. "I don't think the people observing us will panic if we do. They'll probably be expecting it. I'll go."

"No," says Adriana. "I'll go. You two should get to know each other."

After Adriana leaves, Walker says, "Are you surprised about how things are turning out?"

"I don't know what to think," says Louisa.

"Take your time. You don't have to stay if you don't want to. It's up to you."

"Why are you so confident?"

"I'm learning the ways of our family. I'm not that confident, though. Only recently I wandered in just like you did."

"And you stayed."

"Yes."

"Why?"

"I could say I didn't have anywhere else to go and that would be true. But there's more to it. Since I arrived I haven't wanted to go anywhere else."

"Should I stay?"

"I don't think you'll regret it if you do."

Noise erupts from the hallway. The children and some of the adults head upstairs. Adriana,

Celeste, Marcus, Vera, and Smith enter the living room and shuffle the couches and chairs around so they form a rough circle.

Adriana starts by introducing Louisa to everyone and everyone to Louisa. She then summarizes Louisa's warning about the assailants waiting nearby. "Did I leave anything out?" she says.

"They're committed and violent," says Louisa. "They have a sharpshooter poised to kill anyone who tries to escape."

"Such vitriol," says Vera. "Where does it come from?"

"Fear of the unknown," says Adriana. "And they're understandably upset that we managed to escape from their facility."

Walker says, "The question is: how do we respond?"

Louisa says, "I think that if you don't surrender voluntarily they'll come down after you. They most likely think that you've captured and are infecting me."

"The whole idea of infection is so strange," says Celeste.

"Not really," says Adriana. "We know that something happened and now we're unmistakably different. To them it seems like regression; to us it doesn't."

"We could fight them," says Marcus.

"I don't want to hurt anyone," says Celeste.

"Sometimes you have to," says Marcus. "We wouldn't have got out of that place if we hadn't threatened them."

"Yes, but that's all that we did," says Adriana. "The death was an accident. He fell on a needle. But it's true that we're growing and we're going to meet opposition. This is just the first example. What's our attitude going to be about violence?"

"If anyone tries to hurt any of you I'll hurt them first," says Marcus.

"I feel the same way," says Vera.

"I think we all want to protect each other," says Walker. "What Adriana is looking for is some sort of policy. The rules of engagement, so to speak."

"I mean it when I say I don't want to hurt anyone," says Celeste. "I'd rather be hurt instead."

"I think we're missing something here," says Adriana. "We call ourselves a family, but we're actually more than that. Only half our members are human. You know what I mean, don't you?"

Everyone nods except Louisa, who says, "No. I don't know what you mean."

"We'll have to explain it to you later," says Adriana. "I'm wondering, though, if we need to listen more closely to what the other half of our membership thinks."

Celeste says, "We don't know if they even do think, at least independently from us."

"That's true," says Adriana, "and it's going to take time to find out. In the meantime, what do we do about the immediate threat? We're not ready to fight them, and even if we wanted to we have no weapons."

Walker says, "How soon do you think they'll attack, Louisa?"

"I don't know. They'll wait as long as they can. They're afraid of you."

"If we're looking for another location I have a suggestion," says Walker. "Not far from the cabin I was living in is a resort. It seems to be deserted. I walked through the grounds sometimes during my hikes. We could go there. It's isolated. If we can get there without being seen we should be safe. The kitchen might have some food stored, and we can send out teams if we need supplies."

"I agree that we need to go underground for awhile," says Adriana. "And that sounds as good as anyplace. But how do we get there without being seen?"

"We wait until after dark," says Celeste.

"The sun will set in less than an hour," says Vera.

Smith says, "Can I say something?"

"Of course," says Walker. "Go ahead."

"Trying to slip out after dark isn't going to work. The only reason they haven't attacked yet is because they're afraid of us, like Louisa says. I've been trying to think like they would think. What I would do is get closer and move in under cover of darkness. At some sort of prearranged signal they'll jump the wall at various points where they'll have the grounds covered from all angles. I'm talking about the trained militia members. They're the ones we have to be concerned about. And remember: there are only three of them. The facility attendants are untrained, so if they hurt anyone it will be by accident. If we try to escape, the militia will converge on us."

He pauses, but no one interrupts so he continues.

"What we need is a decoy. A diversion. Something to draw away the militia so everyone else can get away unseen."

"What do you suggest?" says Walker.

"The van," says Smith. "Some of us make a big show of starting it up. You know: turning on the lights and revving up the engine. We go slowly enough so that we're sure they're following. We drive down the road, through the city and beyond, and then ditch the van somewhere. When they follow, the rest of us get away clean."

"We don't know that they'll all follow," says Adriana.

"No," says Smith. "But it may confuse them enough to give us a chance."

"Let's do it," says Marcus. "I'll drive."

"I'll go with you," says Smith.

"I'll go too," says Vera. "After we abandon the van, we can make our way to the house where you first found me. When it's safe, you can send someone to show us the way to our new home. If you don't manage to do that, we'll find you somehow."

"I can give you rough directions," says Walker.

"I have a feeling that we'll be able to find one another when we need to," says Adriana. "It's worked so far. So... Is everyone agreed? We'd better start preparing. Some of us can carry backpacks with food and supplies, but let's not overload ourselves. We can find what we need along the way."

Walker says, "I guess this is it. It's time to make a decision. Louisa, are you coming with us?"

"Of course."

VI

He calls himself Nomad. Since he arrived he has traveled up and down this section of coast searching for answers, but mainly he has roamed the city and attempted, with limited success, to access damaged information systems. Now he has deemed it time to locate and confront the lost ones. He doesn't want to attract any attention. Instead of taking the highway, he follows dirt roads and paths and sometimes cuts across country. When he sees individuals or groups of people he avoids confrontations with them. At this point, he wants to be a nonentity. It's not difficult in this shattered society.

He circles around the compound and climbs to a vantage point from which he can observe the activity. Several smaller wooden buildings that appear to be domiciles surround a central larger building. People come and go, engaged in various activities. When they meet one another, they stop and exchange greetings and sometimes hugs. They all appear to be relaxed and self-assured, but Nomad detects an underlying tension.

It is late afternoon. The sun is low over the horizon; its light glitters on the waters of the sea in the distance. The nearby trees cast long shadows.

Three women and two men, obviously weary, hike up the long driveway that zigzags to the resort. When they enter the compound, they head for the central building. A few minutes later, a young girl runs to each of the outlying buildings in turn. People exit them and gather in the center.

Nomad climbs down the hillside, walks to the entrance of the building, hesitates, turns the knob, and enters.

It is a single spacious room with a high wood-beamed ceiling. In the middle of one wall is a stone fireplace with a warm, cheery blaze.

Twelve people are seated on benches at two long wooden tables. In addition, a baby sits in a high chair. They have been laughing, talking, eating, and drinking, but they all pause and stare when they see Nomad.

A dog leaps forward, tail wagging, and projects: *I'm Andy, I'm Andy! Welcome, welcome!*

Nomad understands Andy but doesn't respond apart from crouching down and rubbing Andy's neck.

The tension is almost palpable. They are not sure if Nomad is friend or foe.

"Hello," he says. "My name is Nomad."

A woman stands and approaches. "I'm Adriana. How did you find us, Nomad?"

"I knew where you were."

"How?"

"It's hard to explain. I just knew. I sense that you're suspicious, and you're right to be. People are looking for you. But I'm not a threat."

"I believe you. You're not like us, though. There's something different about you."

"That's right; there is."

"Are you hungry, Nomad?"

"No, thank you, but I'd like some water."

Nomad sits down next to Adriana and sips his water while the conversation resumes around him. The main topic is the successful expedition of Celeste and Sage to bring Marcus, Vera, and Smith back from the coast. Celeste and Sage had left the compound early morning on the previous day, circled around the city, found the others at the mansion with the lighthouse tower, stayed overnight, and then returned with them. When Celeste and Sage finish telling their story, Smith recounts the flight of the multicolored van with three vehicles in pursuit, how Marcus led their would-be assailants on a merry chase through the city's downtown area, veering down one narrow, rubble-strewn street after another in a confusing maze-like pattern until they finally ditched the flamboyant van on a sublevel of a partially demolished parking garage and made their way to the coastal mansion on foot, flitting from shadow to shadow, stopping frequently to observe the way they'd come to be sure that they were not being followed. The stories are all narrated in a spirit of high adventure and punctuated with frequent exclamations, laughter, and applause.

*　*　*

The dishes have been cleared and washed, the tables have been wiped, the floor has been swept, and the benches have been arranged in a semicircle. Nomad, Adriana, Celeste, Travis, Marcus, Sage, Vera, Walker, Lena, Edith, Steve, Smith, and Louisa sit close together facing each other and the fire. Ben nurses at Lena's breast. Andy lies on the floor in the midst.

"Nomad here has something he wants to tell us," says Adriana.

"Yes," says Nomad. "I'm glad that I've found you all and that you have managed to come

110

together. I think that I can help you understand who you are, what has happened to you, and why you are different from other people."

Ben stops nursing and looks intently at Nomad.

"Everyone is different from everyone else," says Lena.

"Of course they are," says Nomad. "And it's obvious that each of you is different in your own ways. Everyone has their own talents, personality, and so on. That's not what I'm talking about. I'm talking about the difference that you all share that has brought you together and that is causing other people to hunt you."

"We're a family," says Travis.

"That concept has brought you together and unified you, which is good," says Nomad, "but it's not exactly accurate. I'm going to explain what really happened to help you understand who you are and decide what you want to do. From a talk I had with Adriana I realize that you've pieced some of it together but it's still not clear in your minds. You can't remember much of your past, can you? None of you can."

No one answers.

"You've spoken to each other of visitors that live inside you. Your assailants call them an infestation. You have a feeling that they're there but you can't communicate with them. You don't really know what they are, do you?"

Again no one answers.

"I'm one of these visitors," says Nomad. "I'm not like you, though; I'm not half and half. I'm full visitor. We come from a far place - far beyond your solar system. Our purpose is exploration and analysis. And in some cases if we find advanced civilizations that need assistance we assist them. We were coming in for a closer look at yours when our vehicle malfunctioned. I'm not sure what happened."

"You crashed," says Travis.

"We crashed, yes," says Nomad. "Usually when we want to conduct close-up observations we create suits that simulate the life-forms we are studying. Like this one." Nomad pats his own chest. "Mine was ready, but the others were not. I escaped in this. As our vehicle disintegrated so did the bodies of my crewmates. They fell and would have been lost in the void, but before they broke apart forever they managed to find something to cling to. You. They fell into each of you and hung on. They are still inside you."

Nomad sighs. "It happened so fast. They couldn't have known what they were falling into or that it would damage your memories when you assimilated them. We are wise beings, compassionate beings. If they had been aware of this, they never would have done it. Even now, if they were self-aware enough to make the decision, they would willingly leave you to restore your wholeness, even if it meant that they would be irreparably lost."

Walker says, "Are you saying, then, that they're not aware?"

"They're partially aware," says Nomad. "I can sense them and they sense me. But they have lost their memories as you have lost yours. The situation seems to be permanent. Separating you, which may not even be possible, would not restore the memories of either."

Walker says, "So whatever we are now is a combination of what we used to be and our visitor."

"Yes," says Nomad. "We possess individuality just as your species does, so no two combinations are alike. We also possess certain skills that most humans don't have. These may become manifest. Some of you may have noticed this."

Adriana says, "The people at that facility called the visitors a contagion. They thought that they could cure us by separating us."

Nomad shakes his head. "It wouldn't have worked. It would have left you imbecilic, or killed you."

"Why should we need a cure?" says Vera. "There's nothing wrong with us."

"You're no longer who you were," says Nomad. "You're different. Humans fear what is different."

"I don't want to change," says Travis. "I have a family. I want to keep my family."

Some of the others murmured their agreement.

"I don't want to separate or change you," says Nomad. "I want to do my best to keep you safe until rescue arrives."

Adriana says, "Rescue?"

"We sent out a distress signal before the vehicle broke up," says Nomad. "Someone will come, although I don't know how long it will take."

Adriana says, "That would be rescue for you. What would it mean for us?"

"I don't know," says Nomad. "This has never happened before."

"I think we need to be more concerned about our present situation," says Walker. "I'm afraid, though, that we don't know exactly what it is."

"I can help you with that, at least partially," says Nomad. "When we arrived, we managed to remain clandestine as we approached your planet. However, as our ship entered your atmosphere and began to break up, it created international news. Since no one knew exactly what was going on, all sorts of rumors began, most of them suspecting something of a military nature. Since your governments had no knowledge of us, they turned against each other. We would have attempted to communicate the truth but we had lost the ability. Wars ensued. Infrastructure got damaged. Many lives were lost. Though brief, it was a terrible, chaotic time. Now, nations are recovering, but slowly. This area where we are presently lacks organization, but it won't last long. The rebuilding effort is ongoing. Progress is slow but steady."

Adriana says, "Do you know who those people are that captured me and hunted us?"

"After I learned that they had attacked you I found out. It's an agency of the fledgling government that suspects an approximation of the truth and has been given limited autonomy to conduct research. You, Adriana, were the first one they found. They hoped to use you as bait to bring in others. When that didn't work, they took a more aggressive approach. They won't stop. They'll continue to hunt you. They consider you a threat."

"We're not a threat," says Celeste. "We just want to be left alone."

"They won't believe that," says Nomad. "Too much has been destroyed. Too many lives have been lost."

"So what do we do?" says Walker.

"I've given it a lot of thought," says Nomad. "In my opinion, you have to go underground. Leave this area. Go far away. My suggestion would be up the coast at least a few hundred miles. Wherever you go you can stay close together if you like; that will be better for me too when I need to find you again. But you'll have to split up for traveling and for day to day living. You need to appear to be traditional family units, not radical communes. People are suspicious. You can't stand out. I realize that your past identities mean nothing to you, but authorities will be tracking you using those criteria. You'll have to get rid of any old official paperwork that you have. I can help you forge new identities with new names."

"Will you come with us?" says Travis.

"I can't. There were others who fell. I think that they may be lost, but I have to keep searching. I'll help you prepare, though, and see you off."

Vera says, "Were there originally forty-nine crewmembers? And were they organized in groups of seven?"

"Yes," says Nomad. "How did you know?"

"I painted it," says Vera.

Nomad looks closely at Vera. "I know who you are."

"What do you mean?" says Vera.

"I recognize the visitor inside you," says Nomad. "In fact, I am beginning to recognize my friends inside all of you. It's comforting and baffling at the same time, because we can't properly communicate."

"Don't you communicate the way we do?" says Travis.

"No," says Nomad. "Not exactly. Some of you, though, can partially communicate our way." He points to Ben. "*He* can." He points to Andy.

"And *he* can. Some of you others have glimmers. In time you may learn more."

Andy wags his tail. *You understand Andy?*

"Yes, Andy," says Nomad. "I understand you."

Andy moves closer to Nomad, his tail wagging wildly. Nomad rubs behind his ears and pats his back.

"There's something wrong with your explanation," says Adriana. "This obscurity of communication... It doesn't make sense. When I left the facility I searched for my family and found them. I knew where they were."

"Yes," says Nomad. "That was *your* group of seven. You were - you are - particularly attuned to them. You're their leader."

"And these others," says Adriana, gesturing with her arm. "Are they another group of seven?"

"Not exactly," says Nomad. "Walker was a group leader, but none of his group is here. Lena, Edith, Steve, and Ben are all part of another group, and this might come as a shock, but Ben was the leader of it. His human aspect is young, but the visitor inside is not. When he's better able to talk he'll probably have a lot to say."

"He... He already has been talking," says Lena. "He's been directing me, telling me where to go and what to do."

"Has he?" says Nomad.

Ben nods solemnly.

"Ah, yes, I see," says Nomad. "For now, though, he's still hungry."

Ben recommences nursing.

Adriana says, "What about Smith and Louisa?"

"They're members of different groups. The only ones I've found in each so far," says Nomad. "You have to understand something. I'm almost as confused as you are. Because I managed to escape in my suit, I have kept my identity and my memories intact. Otherwise I'm like someone in a lifeboat lost at sea after their ship sank. I'm hoping for rescue, counting on rescue. Until then, I want to help as many of us as I can."

"But we aren't your people," says Walker. "Not exactly."

"Yes you are," says Nomad. "You just don't remember. Your species doesn't abandon people who lose their memories, do they?"

Celeste says, "From what I heard in the convent, they do sometimes. That's why the nuns took me in."

*　*　*

Later the assembly breaks up and everyone goes to their cabins. Celeste and Louisa share one with Lena and the children. Walker, Marcus, Travis, and Smith invite Nomad to use an empty bed in theirs. In your cabin, Sage and Vera both breathe the long, slow cadence of deep slumber, but you feel restless. You quietly rise, slip into shoes, put on

118

a jacket, and go outside. Andy accompanies you. The chill air calms and comforts you as you cross an overgrown lawn to a wooden bench from which you can observe the sliver of moon, smattering of stars overhead, and the faint glimmer of the celestial shine on the distant ocean. Andy crawls up onto the bench with you and puts his head on your lap. You reach out with your mind and sense the other five members of your group of seven. You know that those not of your group are nearby too but you can't feel them the way that you feel your own. You consider what Nomad said about the abilities of the visitors. This awareness comes from them, then. And yet you are not quite one of them and not quite human. You are something more. Something new. Nomad's input is valuable; he understands in a limited way, but he is not one of you. Ultimately the fourteen of you are responsible for each other and accountable to no one else. And if you choose to consider yourselves part of a family, then that's what you are. Nomad is probably right about the necessity of moving and changing identity. However, it is imperative that you do it together. The details of the move are inconsequential compared to this reality.

*   *   *

Marcus and Smith are snoring; Travis is silent but deeply asleep. In the darkness, Nomad makes minute adjustments to temperature, sensory input, and other instrumentation on his suit. He

119

doesn't need to sleep but he realizes the efficacy of conforming to local customs, so he settles on the bed and prepares to cycle down to semi-conscious mode. However, he abruptly realizes that someone is outside.

He rises, crosses the room, and slips out the door into the cool moon-silvered night. He makes no effort at silence as he crosses the grassy clearing, as he doesn't want to startle Adriana, who sits cross-legged, eyes closed, on a bench.

"Good evening," says Nomad.

"Good evening."

"I hope I'm not disturbing you."

"No. I've been expecting you, or at least hoping you would come." Adriana opens her eyes and uncrosses her legs. "Come, sit down."

"Thank you."

"I've been thinking about what you've said. You're right. We need to leave this area, and traveling north up the coast is as good a direction as any. You said you can provide identification?"

"Yes."

"I've already given most of them new names. Can you find out what they are and use them?"

"Yes."

"We'll need money."

"Money is easy to get. The information systems have begun to come back on line. It's just a matter of slightly altering the data. I can give you enough to get you started, and I can show you how to take more."

"Isn't that stealing?"

"You'd be surprised how much waste there is, how many dormant pools of money are lying around in data systems. It really doesn't hurt anyone to skim some."

"All right. Don't show me how, though; show Sage or Vera or someone else who has a talent for it."

"I will. There still aren't many vehicles operational, so if you travel by road, you might stand out. Trains are running regularly. I'll get you some tickets."

"Thank you."

"I suggest you leave as soon as possible."

"We will."

After a moment of silence, Nomad says, "You're not planning to split up as I suggested, are you?"

"I appreciate your help," says Adriana. "And I understand that you offer it because your crewmates are trapped in our bodies; but I need to make something clear. We are not yours, and we are not accountable to you or to anyone. We are unique as individuals and as a group, and if we want to find a way to stay together, that decision is ours. Not yours. For your sake I hope your rescue comes. If it does, you are welcome to come and inform us of the situation. But we don't have to come with you. We'll come if we want, and we'll stay if we want. If you can't accept that, don't bother to come looking for us. Do you understand?"

"Yes."

"I don't mean to be abrupt or unkind. I just want to make our position clear."

"Are you speaking for all of them?"

"I haven't put it to them so bluntly yet, but I can say with good confidence that I am."

"I'm going to leave early tomorrow morning to see to the details. While I'm gone, ask them. If they agree with you, I promise to honor your wishes."

Part Three: Answers and Questions

I

The sun has not quite risen but the sky has lightened to a brilliant sapphire through which some of the brighter stars are still visible. The fourteen of them wait with Nomad on a platform for the doors of the train to open up so they can board. Most of them have packs on their backs and some have duffle bags at their feet. Edith holds Celeste's hand, and Steve holds Lena's hand. Ben is fast asleep in his laid back stroller, a blanket tucked over him.

Scattered individuals and other small groups of waiting passengers line the platform, but none are close.

They haven't brought much with them: toiletries, a few articles of extra clothing, and food and drink for the journey. Sage has insisted on keeping a dozen books that she culled from the mansion's library.

Some of the adults are half-asleep and yawning, but Travis is keyed up and excited. He hardly feels the weight on his back. He may have traveled by train in the past, but if he did, he doesn't remember it. This is a first for him. An adventure.

He sidles up closer to Adriana and Nomad so he can hear what they are talking about.

Nomad hands her some slips of paper. "I tried to get you some sleeping suites," he says, "but there were none available. They may not have them in operation. These are twenty seats, all in the same coach car. I booked extra so you have room to stretch out. They go partially back, at least, to help you relax. I hope you'll be comfortable."

"We'll be fine, thank you."

"The trip will take thirty-five to forty hours. You'll arrive tomorrow in the late afternoon or early evening. The station is in the downtown area close to the waterfront. The area suffered some damage but not as much as here. Some shops and hotels have reopened. You should be able to find accommodation while you look around for something more permanent."

"We appreciate all you've done for us," says Adriana.

Nomad nods. "I'd better get going then." He raises his voice slightly. "Goodbye, everyone. Stay safe. I hope we meet again sometime."

Nomad exits the platform.

The train doors hiss open.

"This is our car," says Adriana.

They all climb aboard. No one else enters their car; they seem to have the space to themselves. They stow their baggage in the overhead bins and find seats close to each other. Ben has awakened; he sits on Lena's lap. Steve sits beside them.

Travis sits on the aisle seat next to Edith, who is gazing out the window. She says, "Will we be leaving soon?"

"Yes," says Travis. "We should be."

"I've never been on a train before," says Edith.

Travis's first impulse is to explain to her that she might have been but she doesn't remember, but then he decides that he doesn't want to spoil the moment.

The train lurches once, twice, thrice, and then moves forward, slowly picking up speed.

Edith's eyes widen. She looks at Travis with a big smile, and then turns her attention to the passing scenery: the station, the train yard, the outskirts of the city, and then open country. The train follows the coast, and they have panoramic views of the ocean, the beaches, grasses and scrub lining the shore, and trees with branches that grow only on one side as if they are attempting to flee the winds coming off the sea.

For an hour or so the scenery holds Travis's attention. Vera pulls breakfast out of a pack, and they all feast on nuts, dried fruit, cheese, and bread.

After that, though, Travis becomes impatient. He wants to explore this strange juggernaut that is speeding them northward. He stands and says, "I'm going to look around."

Edith slides out into the aisle and says, "I want to go with you."

Steve hops up and says, "I want to come too."

"I don't know if that's safe," says Lena.

Celeste says, "They should be fine. They can't go far, and the train is enclosed. There's no stop for at least half an hour. I'm sure they'll be back before then."

Ben looks briefly into Lena's eyes.

"I suppose a little exercise will be good for you," says Lena, "but be careful."

"I'll look after them," says Travis. He takes Steve's hand and the three of them move past the rest of the family toward the rear of the train. At the end of the car, Travis has to grip a handle and slide a door open. After they go through, it slides shut behind them, and they find themselves in a space between the cars in which the floor wobbles and the noise of the wheels on the track is uncomfortably loud. Another sliding door brings them into the next car.

This one is sparsely occupied by couples and individuals huddled in isolated clusters with their belongings. Some of them glance at the children as they pass, while others assiduously gaze out the windows. Nobody smiles at them or offers a greeting.

Travis, Edith, and Steve go through the sliding doors into the next carriage.

In the front of this one are disoriented travelers similar to those in the previous car. However, in the rear are about a dozen frightened-looking girls and boys roughly the same age as Edith and Steve. Their clothes are patched and worn. They sit still with their hands on their laps looking furtively up with cowed expressions. Their overseers, a man and a woman who appear as if they have long ago forgotten how to smile, are in aisle seats at the back of the group.

Travis smiles and says hello to the children.

"What do you want?" says the female overseer.

"I was just saying hi," says Travis.

"Where are your parents?" says the woman.

"They're back up the train. We're just looking around."

"Well, move on then," says the woman. "You have no business here."

Travis says, "Are these your children?"

The woman scoffs at the notion. "Ours? Of course not. These are orphans on their way to a facility where they'll be taken care of. Now stop harassing them or I'll call a conductor."

"All right. I'm sorry." As Travis, Edith, and Steve move through the midst of the group, the children cast quick furtive looks at them and then return their gazes to their laps.

After the door has slid shut behind them, in the noisy space between cars, Edith says, "They were scared. Those people aren't their parents. They don't care about them."

"Someone needs to help them," says Steve.

"I feel sorry for them too," says Travis, "but there's nothing we can do. A lot of bad things happen in the world but we can't fix all of it. Do you want to go on or do you want to go back?"

"Let's go on," says Edith.

Steve nods.

The three of them enter the next car.

This one is not a conventional passenger car. There are several benches in the front, and behind these is strapped-down luggage. On the benches sit five men in uniform brandishing rifles, with pistols and truncheons at their belts.

"Militia," says Travis.

"That's right," says one of the men. "And what the hell are you kids doing here?"

"We're just exploring," says Travis.

"Well, this is the end," says the man. "Beyond here there's nothing but baggage. Go on back to your parents. You shouldn't be wandering around by yourselves."

"No need to be rude to them," says another man. "They've done no harm."

"Maybe not," says the first man, "but they should be careful. I lost my own two sons less than six months back, and if I had them with me now I'd watch them like a hawk. These are troubled times. Troubled times."

"You'd better get back to your folks," says the second man. "Go on now."

*   *   *

After the adventure in the rear carriages, Travis is content to stay close to his family. The scenery holds his interest for a long time, but as the day drags on, the monotony of the journey sets in. Edith and Steve briefly fall asleep for a nap, but when they awaken they share Travis's impatience.

Edith says, "Is it much farther?"

"We're going to stay overnight on the train and arrive tomorrow," says Travis. "That's exciting, isn't it?"

"I suppose," says Edith. "So what should we do now?"

Sage comes to the rescue. One of the books she has brought is full of fantasy stories replete with colorful illustrations. She hands it to Travis.

Steve scurries out of his seat to share Edith's. There's plenty of room for both.

On the cover of the book is a fairy tale castle.

On the inside title page is a picture of a knight fighting a dragon.

Travis turns to the first story and begins to read. It's about a poor young man who lives alone at the edge of a village. He yearns to advance his status in life but is too timid to do anything about it. One day a wizard visits him and gives him some magical implements that he says will help the young man fulfill his ambitions. Strengthened by what he perceives as the wizard's magic, the young man travels to a distant land where he combats fearsome monsters and gains a fabulous treasure. When he returns to the village, he marries the woman of his dreams. However, the wizard informs the plucky hero that the implements were not magical at all, and that it was his own wisdom, resolve, courage, and strength that saw him through his many hardships to victory.

Edith and Steve like that story a lot. They discuss how they too are on a quest. They pledge to remain courageous and resolute no matter what the future might hold.

Travis reads several more stories to them while the train churns onward, stopping occasionally at stations where passengers disembark and board. The car in which they sit does not become crowded, though, and no one sits close to them. It is as if their group is protected from incursions from outside by an invisible bubble.

Eventually the sun sets, the outside becomes dark, and the overhead lights dim. Steve returns to his seat next to his mother. After a light supper and trips to the restroom, everyone settles their seats back and closes their eyes.

Travis quickly falls asleep, but his slumber is light. The night passes in fitful dreams and waking moments dominated by the sound and shudder of the train's movement.

In the morning, Travis is sluggish and desultory. So, it seems, is everyone else as well. Time passes in a haze of scenery swiftly flowing by outside the windows accompanied by the hypnotic rhythm of wheels on track. Since boredom and weariness are obviously ubiquitous, nobody complains.

They enter the outskirts of a large city, pass an area full of industries and warehouses, many of which have been partially destroyed, slowly churn through a vast yard where train cars are parked one after another on sidings, and finally come to a stop at a station platform.

II

With packs on backs and duffle bags in hand, they exit the station onto a downtown street. Andy, normally vivacious and eager to explore, remains somber and content to keep pace with the others.

Although not as ostensibly damaged as the city they have come from, this city has the same wounded brooding spirit. Few pedestrians roam the sidewalks, but in the alleys between buildings are numerous makeshift shelters constructed of wood scraps, bricks, cardboard, and plastic. Most of the shops and offices are boarded up, burned out, or full of rubbish, but a few makeshift restaurants and establishments selling canned goods, tools, and other basic supplies are open.

On a corner an old woman has set up a table with some used books on display, and Sage can't help but stop and browse. The others pause and wait patiently for her. A few follow her over to have a look.

"I knew you'd stop," says the proprietor of the open-air stall. "I saw the way your eyes lit up when you saw the books."

"Yes," says Sage. "For a while I lived in a library."

"I live in one now," whispers the old woman.

"Really?"

"Where do you think I got these books?"

"Oh. But don't you want to keep the collection intact?"

"Why? I need money. And besides, this is a way of getting the books into people's hands. I'll let you in on a little secret. If I see that someone is enamored of a book, I give it to them anyway whether they're able to pay for it or not." She smiles broadly, and then says seriously, "But I prefer payment."

"Of course you do," says Sage. "You wouldn't happen to have a guidebook of the area, would you? We just arrived and we're not sure where to go next."

"If you want my advice, don't stay around here," says the old woman. "I'm all right, but many find it depressing. Look for somewhere along the coast on the outskirts of town. Or you could try one of the larger islands. They're lovely and uncrowded, and daily ferry service has resumed."

"That's a good tip," say Sage.

"This might help you," says the woman, pulling a large paperbound book from a box under the table. "It has maps and everything. Go on, take it."

Sage insists on paying for the book. The woman is grateful and gives Sage a hug.

*　　*　　*

The hotel that Nomad booked for them is old but intact. It's located a few blocks away from the waterfront, and since their rooms are on the fourth floor, they have a good view of the harbor. They have three large suites, and they divide them up as they had the cabins at their last encampment: Walker, Marcus, Travis, and Smith in one; Celeste, Louise, Lena, Edith, Steve, and Ben in another; and Adriana, Sage, Vera, and Andy in the third. They leave the doors that connect the various suites unlocked, and since Adriana's suite is in the middle it becomes the point of congregation. While they

133

share food left over from the train ride, Sage sits at a desk and opens the book that she has just purchased. Its information and analyses cover the city itself and the surrounding towns. To the east, populated areas end in a range of lofty mountains. To the west, islands sprinkle a large sheltered bay. Unfortunately the guidebook was written pre-catastrophe. Some of the towns and villages no longer exist or have been abandoned, and some of the roads have been blocked with debris or reduced to rubble. Still, at least Sage and the others are able to get a general idea of the geography and topography.

"We need more details," says Sage. "I'd like to go back and talk to the bookseller again."

"I'll go with you," says Vera.

"I think I should go by myself," says Sage. "I don't want her to become frightened or intimidated."

"We're new here," says Adriana. "We don't know if this area is safe or not."

"It's not far," says Sage, "and I won't stay away long, but this is important. We need this information."

"Let her go," says Walker. "We need to trust each other."

"It's not a matter of trust," says Adriana. "It's a matter of... I suppose I'm just worried. I don't want anything to happen to you."

"I know," says Sage. I'll be careful."

Marcus says to Vera, "You can come with me. I'm going to go buy some groceries."

"I'll come too," says Smith. "I'd like to have a look around."

*   *   *

When Sage reaches the corner where she bought the book, she sees that the seller is packing up. She has collapsed the legs of the table and loaded it and the boxes of books onto a hand truck.

Sage says, "Leaving already?"

"I'm tired," says the woman, "and I've made my quota of cash for the day. I don't like to stay out too long. It isn't safe."

"I was hoping to ask you some questions," says Sage. "I took a look at the book, but it's outdated."

The bookseller studies Sage for a moment. "Would you like to see the library?"

Sage nods.

"Come with me." The old woman starts maneuvering the hand truck down the sidewalk.

"Let me help you."

"I can handle it. I'm used to it. My name is Martha, by the way."

"Sage."

"Nice to meet you. Who were those people you were with?"

"They're my..." Sage stops herself from identifying them as her family; the obvious discrepancies in appearance would provoke a long

135

discussion that she doesn't want to get into. They had agreed enroute that the unusual circumstances that brought them all together would remain clandestine, at least for now. "We've been traveling together."

"It must be nice to have company. I live alone. My daughter and her family are on the other side of the country. I haven't heard from them. I hope they're alright."

Martha turns down a narrow alley that's free of makeshift dwellings and then into an even narrower walkway. She unlocks a nondescript door and pushes the hand truck inside. "Come on," she says.

After Sage enters, Martha locks and bolts the door.

Leaving the hand truck, they traverse a shadowed corridor. "This is the service area," says Martha. "Restrooms, supply room, utilities room, and so on. And here..."

She pushes open a double door and they enter the ground floor of the library. Sunlight shining through tall windows illuminates row after row of shelves brimming with books.

Sage looks around in awe and reverence. Her emotions are similar to those she felt when she used to contemplate the endless volumes in her former home. "It's beautiful," she says.

"Yes," says Martha. "I love to read, but sometimes I walk around, especially at night, and I feel like I'm absorbing something just by being near them. I think that the spirits of the authors live in some of these books. They whisper to me. I hear them."

Sage does not scoff or contradict. In fact, she used to have similar thoughts herself when she lived all alone in the library in the southern city. She walks along an aisle gently touching the spines of the books. Regardless of the specific content, within are words, and perhaps sometimes pictures, that can teach and inspire and edify and encourage and entertain. Even if the books are not actually haunted, they contain the spirits of their authors encompassed in the thoughts that they expressed.

Martha follows quietly behind Sage as she wanders aisle after aisle.

Sage pauses in wonderment. She knows that it's impossible, but it is almost as if she really does hear voices. "Martha, listen," she says. "Is it possible?"

"I'm afraid I haven't been completely honest with you," says Martha. "I'm not alone here. Come with me."

Martha leads Sage up the broad staircase and down a corridor to a door behind which voices can distinctly be heard. "This room used to be used for public events," she says. "It still is, in a sense."

She opens the door, and they enter a room filled with several long tables. A score or more of children of various ages sit at the tables on folding chairs, and about a dozen women sit with them or stand over them. The tables are replete with books, notebooks, loose sheets of paper, pens, pencils, erasers, sharpeners, crayons, and other writing implements and stationary items.

Everyone looks up as the door swings shut.

"Please don't let us interrupt," says Martha. "This is Sage. She's just arrived in the city."

The women and children smile; some mumble greetings; and then they return to what they were doing.

Martha draws Sage aside to a corner where there are spare chairs and whispers, "I was one of the librarians, and when the trouble started I sought shelter here. In the aftermath of the chaos I realized that women and children were the most vulnerable, so I decided to do something about it. Some of them come in the morning and leave before dark, but most of them stay here. They have nowhere else to go. Things are getting more organized and groups of militia are policing the area now, but during the really bad times women were being forced into prostitution and children were rounded up for degrading and dangerous labor."

"I know," says Sage. "It was the same where we came from."

"Where was that?"

Sage tells her.

"Ah, yes," says Martha. "I heard that it was even worse there."

"This is wonderful," says Sage. "You're doing a very good thing."

"Not many schools have opened yet," says Martha, "and none here in the center. The kids need somewhere to go and something to do. I saw that you have children with you. They can come here if you want."

"We're not planning to stay," says Sage. "We're looking for somewhere more remote. That's what you advised us when we first met, remember?"

"That's right; I did."

"The guidebook you gave me was helpful, but I was wondering if you had anything more detailed."

"I'm sure I can find you some other books that describe the area, but they've become rare and valuable. You'll have to return them."

"I will. I promise. I don't suppose you have anything describing conditions after the chaos?"

"I wish I did. A few local printers have resumed operations, but it will take time to assemble and organize that sort of material."

"Of course."

"Still, I pick up snatches of what's happening as I'm working on the streets. I think I can give you at least a rough idea of the information you need. Come."

Martha leads Sage to a smaller room that functions as her office. "I've got a bundle of maps that the library used to distribute to tourists," she says. She unfolds one on her desk and grabs a pen. "We're here," she says, and draws a circle. "Where are you staying?"

Sage names the hotel.

"That's here." Martha draws another circle. "This zone all the way to the harbor has a militia unit on regular patrol so it's fairly safe. There are some dangerous spots nearby that you should avoid, though, like here and here and here." Martha marks one dangerous location after another with a large X. "Here are some places that might be safe and pleasant." She draws larger circles around various positions outside the city and on the offshore islands. "Let's see if we can find more information about these places."

III

Marcus, Vera, and Smith find most of the groceries they are looking for at a shop just a block and a half from the hotel. For some specialty items on their list, though, they have to go three more blocks. As they walk up a hill inland away from the harbor, the ambiance of the neighborhood changes. The streets are dirtier, more windows are smashed in, and pedestrians are more furtive and suspicious.

"I'm glad I'm not alone," says Vera. "I got off my guard down below. This is like a jolt of reality."

"Hopefully more areas will be safe soon," says Marcus. "We can go back to the hotel if you want. We can do without these last few things."

Beyond a low iron fence and an overgrown yard, the door of a dilapidated mansion opens; a woman steps out onto the porch and poses suggestively. After a moment she is joined by another woman, and then by a man. They stare at Marcus, Vera, and Smith as they pass.

Smith stops and stares back.

Marcus calls to Smith and he resumes walking, albeit with many a backward glance.

After the team completes their shopping, the return to the hotel is accomplished without incident. Vera goes inside. Smith pauses at the door, and so does Marcus.

"Can you take the bags?" says Smith. "I don't feel like going upstairs. I think I'll walk around for awhile."

Marcus sets down the bags he has been carrying and contemplates Smith for a moment. "You can't pay for it," he says. "It's not right. You know that, don't you?"

Smith looks as if he is fumbling for something to say but remains silent.

"I used to do it too," says Marcus. "I didn't know any better, but now I do, and so do you. They're not doing it because they want to; they're doing it for the money. They're being forced by circumstance to give up their bodies, but you can't buy their love. It's not supposed to be like that."

"But I miss being with a woman," says Smith. "With the women in our family it somehow doesn't seem right, so I have to find someone else."

"I'm not sure our women are unavailable," says Marcus. "It's just that we've been through one emergency after another and we haven't settled enough for something to happen. In the meantime, you need to try to find women who can also be your friends."

"Do you know how impossible that sounds?"

"Yes. It's frustrating. I'm feeling restless too. We're just going to have to somehow be patient. Come on, let's drop these things upstairs and then go get a drink."

The bar that Marcus and Smith choose is down near the waterfront. The dim interior lighting contrasts with the clear afternoon light outdoors. In one corner two men sit with several women. At other tables scattered around the room, couples and small groups of men sit quietly talking as they drink.

Marcus and Smith take barstools at the counter and order beers.

It isn't long before two women break loose from the corner cluster and approached them. "Hello," says one. "I'm June."

"Hello, June," says Marcus.

"And this is Rose."

"Hi," says Smith.

Rose says, "Would you like to buy us a drink?"

Marcus gestures towards the corner. "It looks like you're already with friends. We don't want to interrupt."

Rose says, "If we wanted to stay with them we'd still be there."

"Well, maybe it's better that you go back there," says Marcus. "We're just going to drink our beers and then go."

The two women return to their group and whisper intently to the men.

"You're right," says Smith. "They're attractive, but I don't feel the same way I used to. Something's changed."

Before Marcus can respond, the two men who have been sitting with the women get up and approach. One says, "My ladies Rose and June say you've been disrespecting them."

"No disrespect intended," says Marcus. "They invited themselves for a drink but we said we didn't want to disturb your company."

"Disturb our..." the man chuckles mirthlessly. "What the hell are you talking about? You seriously don't know what's going on here?"

"Of course we know," says Marcus. "And we declined as politely as we could. Now one of two things will happen here. You can abide by our decision and go back and relax with your friends, or this can all get messy. I have trouble remembering my past sometimes, but I *do* recall a few bloody bar fights that ended in busted skulls and broken limbs. Your choice. Are you sure the owner would take kindly to us trashing his establishment?"

The man and Marcus stare at each other for a moment. "Man, *I* own this place. But I like you." He smiles again, this time genuinely. To the bartender he says, "Give these two another round on the house."

As the owner walks away, Marcus calls out, "Hey!"

The man turns.

Markus says, "From what I hear, the war is over. I'd like to keep it that way."

As Marcus and Smith are walking back to the hotel, Smith says, "I don't see how you did that. I thought that for sure we were in for a brawl."

"I don't know what happened," says Marcus. "Before I met Adriana and the family, I would have hit first and asked questions later. Something's changed. I hardly knew what I was saying."

"I want to get out of the city," says Smith. "I want to go somewhere quiet and uncomplicated."

IV

Adriana, Walker, Vera, and Louise are sitting at a table listening to Sage explain the details on the map she has brought back when Marcus and Smith return.

"Did you have a good time?" says Adriana.

"It was an unnecessary risk," says Marcus. "We almost got into a bar fight."

"Maybe it's better for us to keep a low profile for now," says Walker. "We don't want to draw attention."

"Sorry," says Smith.

"There's no need to apologize," says Adriana. "You're adults. You can do what you want - although in my opinion Walker is right."

"Of course he is," says Marcus. "Did you find anything?"

"Martha made a few suggestions," says Sage, "and I brought some more printed information. We're just going through the options now." Marcus and Smith look over shoulders as Sage continues. She indicates three locations. "These seem to be the best possibilities."

"It's a big step," says Adriana. "We have to be sure."

"We can send out scouting teams," says Smith. "One to each area. I'll go."

"I agree with having a look before we all move," says Walker, "but I'm not sure about sending multiple teams to unknown places. I know we're anxious to be gone, but we should also be cautious."

"Walker's right," says Vera. "We're going into the unknown. We should take it step by step."

"If we only send out one team, where should they go?" says Adriana. "Maybe we should call everyone for a vote."

After a general summons everyone, including children, crowds into the room. Adriana explains that they need to decide where to start looking for their new home.

Sage tells what she knows of the three locations. They are all approximately the same geographical distance away, but in different directions. One is near a town beside a lake due north of where they are. Another is to the east: a forested area at the edge of a mountain range. "It would be colder there, with more snow in the winter," says Sage. "But it would be pretty in the midst of the evergreens, and we could find a place on a hillside somewhere with a spectacular view." The third place is on a large island across the water to the west. "A ferry runs twice a day from the city to the island's largest town on its east side. The location Martha suggested is on the west side of the island along a strait that separates the island from a large peninsula of the mainland. Some people may still be in the area, but Martha thinks probably not many. When we need supplies, we can obtain them from the town near the ferry terminal."

"So those are the places we have been considering," says Adriana. "There may be others, but we have to start somewhere. While the team is looking at the site we choose, we can do more research and gather a few supplies for setting up our new home. The question now is: where do we go first? Everyone think about it for awhile, and when you're ready, we'll vote."

It didn't take long for people to make up their minds. Adriana called out names, and Walker marked the tally on a piece of paper. Even the children were allowed to state their preference, and Lena announced Ben's decision, which turned out to be different from her own.

"It's not even close," says Walker. "The island is the clear winner."

"And now we need to choose the team," says Adriana.

"I want to go," says Smith.

"I want to go too," says Louisa.

No one else raises a voice.

"You know, I was going to suggest you two," says Walker. "I'm not even sure why."

"So was I."

"And me."

"I was too."

"There's some strange dynamic about this," says Adriana with a smile. "I don't quite understand it either, but the decision seems to be unanimous."

Ben nods and smiles.

Andy barks and wags his tail.

V

The ferry ride to the island is spectacular. Louisa and Smith spend most of the time out on the open deck admiring the bright blue sky, darker blue waters, deep green overlay of the evergreen forest on the island, and distant snow-covered mountain range. In contrast, the buildings on the skyline of the city behind them look like the broken teeth in the jawbone of a monstrous skull. Overhead white gulls swoop and screech; sometimes they settle down onto the ferry's wake and bob about like plastic toys. The dense chill air smells of salt and fish and seaweed drying on beaches. There are only two vehicles onboard, a delivery van and a pickup truck loaded with tools and bundles, and less than two dozen passengers. Everyone else remains within the warm interior, so Louisa and Smith have the deck to themselves.

Once they land, they spend little time exploring the town on the island's east side. After renting bicycles, they buy some food and drink, which they carry in saddlebags on the rear of the bikes. They then set out to the northwest on a lonely highway. There are no cars, vans, or trucks on the road, although they occasionally glimpse vehicles parked in the driveways of deserted homes surrounded by overgrown lawns and gardens. Between pockets of housing they pass stretches of forest in which tall evergreens with thick trunks cluster close together and lean into one another. Below the trees are moss-coated logs, dense underbrush, pockets of ferns, and tangled thorn-filled berry bushes.

The waters of the strait and the peninsula beyond become visible off and on through the trees to the left of the highway. When they spot a sign indicating a village to the west, Louisa and Smith turn off onto a smaller two-lane asphalt road.

The village consists of about two dozen scattered houses and a single short block lined with shops, all of which are closed and some of which have shattered windows and flamboyant graffiti on their exteriors. At the end of the street are a short wooden dock and a deserted public beach. In fact, the entire village seems to be deserted.

After stopping and dismounting at the edge of the dock, Smith says, "Where is everyone?"

"It's like down south," says Louisa. "People have congregated in the more populated centers because that's where they can find supplies. Plus they're probably frightened of being too isolated. The outlying areas are deserted. That's not a bad thing for us."

"Won't we have trouble getting supplies too?"

"We can work something out. It's pretty here, isn't it?"

"It's beautiful."

They look around at the reflection of the landscape on the calm water and the profusion of greenery on shore.

As they shift their gazes to the silent buildings behind them, they become aware of a solitary old man on a chair in front of an easel on a lawn a few hundred yards away. He holds a brush in one hand and a palette of paints in the other. He has noticed them too and regards them with a mix of surprise and serenity.

Louise and Smith walk their bikes over, use the kickstands to prop them up on the sidewalk, and mount a slight slope to where the man sits. He has long gray hair and a luxuriant gray beard and is dressed in blue pajamas, a darker blue robe, and green cloth slippers.

The man stands up and sets down his painting implements on the chair as Louisa and Smith approach. "I apologize for my attire," he says, "but I wasn't expecting visitors. My name is Alfred Lake." He shakes Smith's hand and then Louisa's.

"I'm Smith."

"I'm Louisa."

"Pleased to meet you."

"We haven't seen anyone else," says Louisa. "How many people still live here?"

Lake smiles. "One. Me. I'm alone. Everyone else left months ago. I don't know exactly how long; I've lost track of the time. The other locals heard of violent gangs roaming the countryside looting and killing. They'd made it this far north on the peninsula there; we saw the light of fires across the water. They could have come over the bridge on the north side of the island but they never did. I was stubborn. I love my home and I didn't want to leave. I kept expecting everyone to come back but so far no one has. After this long, I don't know if they ever will."

Louisa asks, "How have you survived here?"

"I had a store of food and water in my basement," says Lake. "That lasted me for months. When I emerged back into the sunlight and realized that the danger had passed, I started painting again. I take my paintings into town and barter them for what I need. A woman has set up a gallery and occasionally sells one for cash. All my life I've wanted to be a full-time artist, and it took an apocalyptic event to make it happen."

"Amazing," says Smith.

Lake says, "You're not in a hurry, are you? Come up to the house and I'll make some coffee."

On a spacious patio, Louisa and Smith sit on metal chairs at a round metal table with a large closed green umbrella in the middle while Lake disappears into the modest single-story white house. He soon emerges with a tray bearing three steaming cups of coffee and three chocolate chip cookies.

"Thank you," says Louisa.

Smith, after biting into a cookie, says, "This is good."

"I'm not much of a cook," says Lake. "These are from a bakery in town."

Louisa says, "Do you get all your food from town?"

"Oh, no," says Smith. "I have a vegetable garden back behind the house, and it's easy to catch fish either from shore or from a rowboat. I still have some canned goods and dry goods in the basement. I haven't taken to looking for food in the homes of my former neighbors or in the local shops, but I could probably do that as well. I'm fairly sure I could get by if I had to even if I couldn't shop in town."

"I don't think many people would be as content as you are to stay here all alone," says Smith.

"That's their loss," says Lake. "I appreciate neighbors if I have them, but I can live without them. Sometimes I crave the company of another person when I'm marveling at a brilliant sunset, for example, but... You know, there's a difference between solitude and loneliness."

The three of them sip coffee in silence for awhile.

"We're looking for a place to live," says Louisa.

"Just you two?" says Lake.

"Actually, no," says Louisa. "We're traveling with a few families. We need somewhere quiet, uncrowded, without disturbances."

"You've come to the right place," says Lake. "To the north and especially to the south of here along the strait is one home after another, each with its plot of land and waterfront access. And they're all empty, as far as I know. I don't think the owners are coming back. You can claim a few if you need them. If you want to do it officially, there's even an office in town where you can register squatter's rights. That puts you on the map for when mail service is restored."

"What if the owners come back?" says Smith.

"That's unlikely," says Lake. "They've probably either been killed during the war or migrated to another area. Right now, though, there's plenty of space for everyone."

*   *   *

Louisa and Smith leisurely ride their bikes south along a narrow paved road that runs parallel to the strait. Every few hundred yards, gravel or dirt driveways to the right lead to private homes. However, most of the houses have been built behind stands of trees so that they are hidden from view by passers-by on the road. To get a good look and ascertain that the dwellings are empty, they'll have to turn into the individual lanes and get closer. First, though, they put a few miles of distance between

153

their prospective home and Alfred Lake. Not that they didn't find the old man friendly and hospitable, but they're looking for a place as isolated from neighbors as possible.

So far no vehicles have passed them on the road, and they've seen no people. A good sign.

"I think we've gone far enough," says Louisa. "Let's try this one."

They turn onto an uneven unpaved lane that winds around a few tall cedars trees and soon come to the remains of a two-story house with attached garage. A fire has consumed about half the home leaving an open gash in one side and in the roof. The exterior was originally yellow, but large swaths of the paint have blistered and peeled, and the edges of the burn are ruinous black. The remains that still stand sag inward toward the gutted fire-decimated center. Rusted appliances and decaying furniture can be seen inside.

Louisa and Smith get off their bicycles and walk closer.

"This didn't happen recently," says Smith. "Look: there are moss and ferns growing inside. Do you think looters did come this way? Maybe Lake missed seeing them because he was hiding in his basement."

Louisa says, "It's impossible to tell. If looters did it, why did they bypass Lake's village? Anything could have happened. Maybe the former residents left something turned on when they fled."

"If it was looters," says Smith, "it may be hard to find anything intact in this area."

They walk over the unkempt lawn towards the water. "It's a shame," says Louisa. "This place is so pretty."

"It is, yes."

"Look!" says Louisa, pointing.

To their left beyond a hillside covered with tall grass, bramble, and young trees, is a russet-colored cabin that appears to be intact.

"Let's go see," says Louisa.

They hop onto their bikes and exit the driveway of the fire-damaged house. A short distance down the road, they turn into the next driveway. A wooden platform with several mailboxes mounted on it lies broken under some bushes. The winding driveway is soft with the matting of fallen evergreen needles. Tall trees on either side cast cool shadows.

When they emerge into sunlight they see the first house on the right. It's a single-story white structure sitting behind a lush overgrown garden that appears in the past to have received tender loving care. To the side and to the rear of the house is an expansive lawn.

"This is more like it," says Smith.

"Come on," says Louisa. "There are more."

Just ahead to the left is the second house. This one is narrower but has two stories. It is painted light blue, and its lawn seems to go all the way down to the water's edge.

To the right a short driveway leads to the russet cabin they had spotted earlier. It is also a waterfront property. It's slightly smaller than the others but, like the others, appears to be pristine.

"Wow," says Smith. "Three houses. Perfect."

"They look good, don't they?" says Louisa. "Of course we'll have to check them out more carefully, but these might be just what we need."

The late afternoon sun is low in the sky to the west, casting long shadows over the landscape.

"It's getting a bit chilly," says Louisa. "Let's see if we can get into this one."

They lean their bicycles against the cabin porch.

Smith tries the door. "Locked," he says.

They move clockwise around the cabin. In the front facing the water is a spacious deck that runs the length of the house. Sliding glass doors lead into the living room and into a bedroom beside it, but they won't budge when Smith tries to push them open. Continuing around to the side, they come to a bathroom window. It's closed, but it yields as Smith nudges it. "Here," he says. Once he opens it all the way, he says, "It's kind of small, but I think you can manage it."

"Me?"

"I don't think I would fit through."

"All right."

"Put your foot in my hands. I'll hoist you up. The toilet might be right under the window. Be careful you don't damage it when you drop."

"How about damaging myself?"

"You'll be all right. Just take it slow and easy."

Smith hoists Louisa up until her elbows are on the sill. Louisa then uses Smith's shoulder to kick herself forward until her upper body is inside. Once this is accomplished, she manages to turn so that she can sit on the sill and slowly lower herself feet first into the room.

After Louisa has unlocked the front door so that Smith can enter, they take a tour by the light of the late afternoon sun flooding through the windows on the west side. Besides the large living/dining room, there are two bedrooms, a storage/laundry room, the bathroom, and the kitchen. Dust covers all surfaces and mold creeps across the ceilings and down some of the walls.

"I like it," says Louisa. "It can be cleaned up, and painted if necessary."

"Should we stay here tonight?" says Smith.

"Why not? It will be dark soon. Better to inspect the other houses in the light of day."

"Water is flowing in the taps, but there's no power. We should start a fire and see if we can find candles before it gets dark."

A metal tub full of kindling sits beside the stone fireplace, and Louisa finds matches on the mantle and candles and holders in a cupboard drawer. Smith carries in an armload of firewood from a shed outside.

While Smith gets a fire going, Louisa searches through the kitchen cabinets. "There's food," she says. "Lots of it. And wine. Let's cook something delicious and celebrate."

Together they commence boiling pasta and warming up tomato sauce from a jar. They open a bottle of red wine and sip it while they work. By the time the meal is ready the sun has set, and they eat by candlelight while they watch the last flamboyant traceries of rose and amber light fade over the forest across the strait.

"I could live here," says Smith.

"The others will love it," says Louisa. "Think how much fun it will be when everyone arrives. There will be so much to do, so much to experience."

"Do you want some more wine?"

"Yes please."

"Do you ever think about your visitor? Doesn't the idea of carrying around another being inside you seem strange sometimes?"

Louisa shrugs. "It did at first. I suppose I've become used to it by now."

"Still... I feel like lately it's been trying to communicate with me more. Has that been happening to you?"

"Maybe a little. What has it been telling you?"

"Well, first of all, I don't think of it as an *it*. I might be projecting, but I think of it as a *him*."

"You think that your visitor is male?"

"I don't think that they have genders like we do. Like I said, I think I'm projecting. I'm male, so I think of what's inside me as male."

"I do the same. I mean that I think of my visitor as a female."

"So does she speak to you?"

"I asked you first."

"I don't know if I should tell you. And anyway, there's this projection thing. Sometimes I can't tell which thoughts are mine and which are his."

"Tell me and we'll sort it out together."

Smith takes Louisa's hand. "How should I put this? I feel attracted, and he feels curious. I've had this on my mind for some time now, but I hesitated to share it because... Well, you know: we talk so much about being a family; I wasn't sure if it was proper to get physical."

"Get physical? How romantic."

"You know what I mean, don't you? I don't think I'm the only one who's felt this kind of tension."

"Of course not. I've felt it too. Do you know one thing that's made me hesitate? The thought of the aliens inside us observing it all like some sort of ethereal Peeping Toms. I suppose we have to get past that, though."

"If we don't we're going to become very frustrated."

"It's getting chilly. Why don't we bring a mattress out here in front of the fire?"

They drag out a mattress and find clean and neatly folded, although slightly musty-smelling, sheets and a blanket in a closet.

At a certain point, after they disrobe and are well into fondling one another, they completely forget about the observant aliens that have taken up residency in their bodies. As they have sex, they sense curiosity, astonishment, and ultimate approval that seem to come from their unseen audience.

When they've finished and are side by side on the mattress, Smith says, "Did you feel that?"

"Of course I felt it," says Louisa.

"I don't mean... You know..."

"Yes, I felt that too."

"This is going to take some getting used to."

"Undoubtedly."

"I wonder if they're having trouble reacting to this situation."

"I'm sure they are. They're supposed to be like Nomad, completely in control of a physical construct. Instead, they've landed in us."

"Are you saying we're inferior?" Smith frowns. "I'm offended."

"Of course not, but just think about it. Imagine if it had happened to us. How would you feel if your spirit, complete with your personality as it is, suddenly fell into someone else's body. You know what's going on around you through the body's senses, but you have no control over where you go or what you do. Or at least very limited control."

"It would be strange."

"It would be more than strange. It would be frustrating and limiting, almost as if you were in prison. You would want to... Wait a minute."

"What?"

"I have that feeling again. I think she's trying to speak through me."

"She? Your visitor?"

"She may be a visitor, or she may be a permanent resident. We don't know yet. I think they're hoping that when Nomad's rescue arrives that some way will be found to separate us. In the meantime, we share exactly the same goals. We want to survive, stay healthy and safe, and enjoy life as much as we can. They want to help. They want to bond closer with us so that they can use whatever strengths they have to accomplish our plan, to protect and nurture the community."

"I've never heard you talk like that before. Adriana sometimes, but not you."

"I know. She's been aware of this longer than I have. I think our lovemaking had something to do with it. It opened a channel somehow. And now I think the best thing to do would be to widen and deepen that channel. Let's take it slow, though. As if we're doing it for the first time. Go through all the steps; build up to it."

"Is that you or her speaking?"

"It's her, I think. Does it matter? Are you up for it?"

"You can see that I am."

They continue their communication by touch. As Louisa has suggested, they go slowly. Unlike the first time, when they are about to reach simultaneous climax they open their eyes and gaze fervently at one another. Their expressions show the orgasm building, building, building... When they come they are absolutely absent of pretenses and cover-ups; they are truly naked.

Afterwards they lie silently together in each other's arms as the fire glows and crackles and dies down and the room darkens into benevolent shadows. For the present, the four of them have melded into a unity beyond words as Louisa and Smith drift off into sleep.

VI

As Walker and Travis enter the shop, a bell above the door rings. In the spacious display room, paintings, most of which depict local landscapes, line the walls, and other works of art, mainly wood carvings, are arranged attractively on tables.

As they wait, Walker and Travis contemplate the various pieces.

"These are nice," says Travis.

"Yes, most of them manifest respect and love for the regional terrain, flora, and fauna," says Walker. "I hope the proprietor likes our more unusual offerings."

A middle-aged woman emerges from a back room.

"Hello," Walker says. "Are you Hailey Benford?"

"That's me."

"We've been recommended to you by a neighbor: Alfred Lake."

"I didn't think Lake had any neighbors."

"We're new," says Walker. "And I'm using the term loosely. We live a few miles from his village."

Hailey smiles. "Lake is not among the better artists on the island, but he works at it and he's improving. I display a few of his pieces now and then as a favor."

"We've set up an artist colony ourselves," says Walker. "We were wondering if you would mind considering some work from a few of our people. I'm Walker, by the way, and this is Travis. He's one of the artists."

Hailey smiles again and nods. "I don't guarantee anything, but I'd be happy to have a look at what you've got."

"They're on the backs of our bikes," says Walker.

"I'll go get them," says Travis.

"Business is slow," says Hailey. "Most people are more concerned with survival than aesthetics."

"Understandable," says Walker.

"Still, I sell some pieces now and then," Hailey says. "I can't charge much for them. I'm more concerned with reviving interest in local art than in making a profit."

"Of course," says Walker. "We *are* hoping, though, that we can at least bring in some funds to help us purchase supplies. And, of course, we want to share what we have created."

Travis returns with two canvas duffle bags.

"Come over here to the counter," says Hailey. She switches on an additional overhead light.

Walker first pulls out an abstract painting replete with flamboyant colors that range from deep blue and purple to red, orange, yellow, and the near-white of starlight.

Hailey looks at it, and then looks closer. She moves the painting around in the light. "It seems to be flames," she says, "or currents of light or air. And as I shift perspective, I catch glimpses of beings like spirits flitting in and out of sight. Impressive."

"That's one of Travis's," says Walker.

"Well done," says Hailey. "I like it."

Walker next shows her a picture with sharper definition depicting a ruined city on the left; on the right is a group of people with glowing auras gazing up at descending celestial vehicles.

Hailey is speechless for a time as she studies it.

"A woman named Vera painted that," says Walker.

"This is..." says Hailey. "This is about..." She sets the painting on the counter. "Nobody I know has done any work on this theme. I've heard of some people on the mainland who are interpreting recent history but I don't have any examples."

Walker says, "Does it disturb you?"

"Yes," says Hailey, "but that's not necessarily a bad thing."

"We brought one more piece today," says Walker. He opens the other duffle bag. "We built a frame around it for protection. Here it is." He lifts out an intricate landscape with a carved wood base and numerous small pieces of carved driftwood comprising landscape features and suggestions of animals, plants, and people.

Again Hailey stares without speaking. After a long silence, she says, "I don't know what to say.

Several people around here do driftwood sculptures, but I've never seen anything like this."

"So you'll display our works?"

"Of course," says Hailey. "Do you have more?"

"Yes," says Walker. "We have more ready now. We brought these smaller ones as samples because we came by bicycle. If we reach an agreement, we'll figure out a way to safely move some of the larger pieces."

"I'll have to check them for quality," says Hailey, "but I don't anticipate that being a problem."

"If you like these it won't be," says Walker.

"They don't fit in with the regional work," says Hailey. "I'll have to clear a dedicated space."

Walker says, "I'll leave that up to you. Keep in mind that some of the already-completed pieces are three to five times larger than the paintings and sculpture you see here. And there will be a lot more of them. We'd like to consider this an ongoing arrangement. You can act as our agent and take whatever commission you consider standard."

"Not many people live out here," says Hailey, "and our island gets few visitors. My artwork moves very slowly."

"I have a feeling it will pick up," says Walker. "Art always inspires people. Making sense out of what's happening to us is a need almost as acute as food and shelter. Maybe you should consider establishing a contact on the mainland that can open a gallery there."

"You've got a lot of confidence, haven't you?"

"There's nothing wrong with positivity. Besides, you've seen our samples. Don't you think our confidence is justified?"

Hailey studies the two paintings and the sculpture arrayed on the counter. "Yes. Yes, it is."

"We'll leave the pricing up to you," says Walker, "but I suggest that you set the base price high." He points to Travis's painting. "For example, this piece you should list for at least..." He names a figure.

"No one will be able to afford that," says Hailey.

"Maybe not," says Walker, "but at least they'll get an initial impression of what it's really worth. After that, you can negotiate. When it comes down to it, we'll be willing to accept food and other supplies, but we'll have to give final approval to any arrangements for barter. Someone will come into town for shopping and to bring you new work at least once a week."

"So often? Some painters around here take months to finalize one picture."

I did that one in a day," says Travis.

"You did?"

"Sure. I think it's a matter of focus, but I suppose everyone works differently. It took them longer to carve and assemble the wood."

"I can imagine that it did," says Hailey.

"There's one other thing," says Walker. "We would appreciate it if you would keep our specific location confidential. We'll come to you; we don't want people coming to us. You are our liaison with the public."

"We've just met. How do you know you can trust me with this?"

"I'm a good judge of character," says Walker. "I can sense your sincerity."

"He's right," says Travis. "You'll do just fine."

VI

Celeste, Lena, Edith, Steve, and Ben have appropriated the single-story white house with the spacious lawn. In one bedroom, Celeste and Lena sleep on a double bed and Ben sleeps nearby in a makeshift crib; in the other bedroom are twin beds for Edith and Steve. Most of the living room has been converted into a studio. Although they clean up as best they can every evening, wood dust and crumbs of wood have infused into cracks in the floor, walls and windows and into the furniture upholstery. The formal dining table has become a work table; they eat at a smaller linoleum-covered table in the kitchen. They have assembled tools for intricate woodcarving from the garages and utility rooms of all three houses; these sit out in ready array. In a corner driftwood of various shapes and sizes is stacked. For the foundations, Marcus has sawed and sanded large rough slabs; several of these are stacked in another corner.

The piece that is presently being worked on sits in the center of the table with several additions already attached. The team sits around the table on benches. Celeste, Edith, and Steve each shape different figures while Lena, prompted by Ben, offers guidance.

Adriana sits next to Lena observing. "Every time I watch them work I'm amazed."

"Don't call it work," says Lena. "It's not work to them. It's not play either. It's something that goes beyond those activities. They love it."

"They *do* get out to play sometimes, don't they?"

"Every day for an hour or more. Celeste and I insist on it. We're going to start teaching a few hours of school in the mornings too as soon as we accumulate the books and supplies."

"This is the topography of their home world, isn't it?"

Ben looks at Adriana and nods.

Adriana says, "Aren't you concerned that the kids will cut themselves with the sharp tools?"

"I was at first," says Lena."As it turns out, the children are more adept at this than Celeste or any other adult who's made an attempt. I share general guidelines, but when they do the intricate work they are able to synch in with Ben's thoughts. He's an expert and helps to direct their movements."

"And you, Celeste?"

"I'm getting better, but my adult human sensibilities get in the way. I pick up impressions from Ben, but they're not sharp. I make far more mistakes than Edith and Steve do."

Lena says, "Edith, make the stems narrower and more veins in the leaves."

Edith pauses for a moment. Before she resumes, she nods at Ben, not at Lena.

Adriana glances up at the large picture window and sees Walker and Travis pass by along the driveway on bicycles. "Oh," she says. "Walker and Travis are back. I'll go see how it went."

After kissing Lena and Ben on their cheeks and waving to the others, Adriana hurries down the road to the light blue house, where Walker, Marcus, Travis, Vera, and Sage stay. Andy, who has been napping under the sculpture table, runs ahead and greets the cyclists with barks, tail-wags, and thought impressions: *Hello, hello! Welcome back!*

Walker and Travis are in the garage removing saddle bags full of supplies and the unwieldy wooden platforms that had held artwork on their way into town from the back of the bikes.

When Adriana approaches Travis says, "Hi! We need to improve the design of these things. They sway as we ride. In a strong wind they would be dangerous."

"I'm sure you and Marcus can streamline them," says Adriana.

"I'm thinking of designing carts that can go behind the bikes."

"Why don't you ask at the bicycle shop the next time you go back into town?" says Adriana. "They may already have something like that."

"I will," says Travis.

"The exchange went well," says Walker. "The three pieces we left there on the first trip sold very quickly and at top prices. Hailey loved the new artwork and promised to display it prominently. She's already been in touch with a dealer she knows on the mainland. She's planning to send him a few of the new pieces."

"Things are moving fast," says Adriana.

"Yes."

"At some point someone is going to make a connection."

"Yes. We've talked about this. Hopefully it won't be too soon; the authorities have a lot more immediate problems than us to worry about. We'll continue to prepare our contingency plans for emergencies. In the meantime..." Walker puts his hand on Adriana's shoulder and smiles. "Relax.

Enjoy yourself. Don't let the burden of responsibility get you down."

"I'll try. Thanks, Walker."

"Travis and I will distribute these things to the homes now. We'll see you later."

Adriana and Andy follow the dirt path that leads from the blue house down to the water. To the left beyond an overgrown lawn is a stand of evergreen trees; to the right past more lawn is the russet-colored cabin where Adriana, Andy, Louisa, and Smith live. Before reaching the shore, the path zigzags down the face of a shallow bluff. The base is reinforced with a concrete platform, and extending from the platform is a small private wooden dock. At low tide the water recedes beyond the dock, but at high tide the dock can be used to launch small boats. A shed on the platform houses two rowboats, oars, and fishing tackle.

One of the rowboats is missing. Far to the south, in the midst of the strait, Adriana spots it. That would be Marcus and Sage out on a fishing run. Sometimes they come back empty, but more often they return with several large fish: cod, flounder, halibut, sole, red snapper, and sometimes salmon.

Andy takes off joyously down the beach, running, sniffing at clam holes, rolling in seaweed, leaping into the sea, swimming in circles, and then vigorously shaking off the water when he comes out. He invariably reeks of mud and other foul odors when they return topside, so Adriana gives him a rinse-down with the hose before letting him back into the house.

Now, today, she's happy to see him play. All appears to be going well with the family community. They have found shelter and a means of support in a beautiful quiet location. They are all getting along well, which is amazing for a group of such disparate individuals.

As Adriana considers the artwork that the buyers in town are so enthralled with, though, she muses that it all depicts the fantasy world of their visitors, either in realistic or abstract form. And yet here before her she is confronted with one of the most beautiful landscapes on Earth: rippling blue waters, deep evergreen forests, sharp distant mountains, and rose and gold shadings painted on the clouds by the sun low on the horizon. She watches Andy cavorting about celebrating the perfection of the surrounding environment and wonders why no one else, particularly the artists, seems to notice it. They are preoccupied, every one of them. It is almost as if now that they have reached a secure location the aliens within them have relentlessly set them to a task. But what's the ultimate purpose of it?

Adriana sighs and shakes her head. *Paranoia*, she thinks. *All the running and hiding is making me paranoid.*

Andy runs up to her. *Happy! Happy! Andy is happy!*

"You like it here, don't you?"

Yes! Room to run! Place to swim! Family! Yes!

The distant boat slowly approaches as Marcus plies the oars.

Adriana focuses her attention to the visitor within her. "I know you're there," she says, "but I don't know how much of what you understand when I speak to you. I'm going to try anyway. We've sacrificed a lot for you. We've given up the memories of who we used to be, and we may never be able to get them back. We are two beings, two life-forms inhabiting the same body. In my opinion, we need to somehow learn to work together. Until now we've been reacting to circumstances, but going forward we need to be proactive. I can't help but think that if we communicate more efficiently we'll be able to do more than we can at present. Let's look at the artwork, for example. Is it intentional on your part that everything our people are producing is about your world, or are they being subliminally inspired by you by the coincidence of your proximity? How can we know these things?"

She pauses, and listens, and feels alone. There is no response, or at least none that she can comprehend.

It occurs to her, though, that it might go better if everyone gets together and attempts communication. She envisions a family meeting in which all are in attendance, both humans and visitors. Nomad indicated that each has different skills and roles, so unity might bring these out.

The sun has nearly reached the horizon; the twilight colors intensify.

Marcus and Sage spot Adriana and Andy on the beach and wave. As they approach the dock, Sage throws a rope to Adriana; she catches it, pulls in the boat, and ties it up.

"Look!" says Sage.

In the bottom of the boat are half a dozen fish, including two large salmon.

"Can you help us carry them up?" says Marcus. "Here, just grab under the gills."

Adriana, Sage, and Marcus each carry two fish up the zigzag path. Andy runs ahead.

Before heading to the russet house, Adriana says, "What do you think about getting together after dinner? All of us, I mean."

"It sounds great," says Sage.

"Could you pass it on to the others?"

"We'll tell them," says Marcus. "Where shall we meet? Our house? Your house?"

"Maybe your house," says Adriana. "It's in the middle. See you soon."

*　*　*

In the fireplace flames gnaw wood and engage in a flickering dance. On side tables in the corners shaded lamps glow. On a coffee table in the

175

center of the group are glasses filled with various drinks: wine, beer, juice, water. Everyone is present: Adriana, Andy, Celeste, Travis, Marcus, Sage, Vera, Walker, Lena, Edith, Steve, Ben, Smith, and Louisa.

"I called you all here tonight because I don't know what to do," says Adriana. "I don't know if we can come up with any answers. I don't know if there *are* any answers, but I wanted to share my thoughts." She pauses as firelight amidst shadows and lamplight causes the room to pulse and shimmer. "We've been running and hiding. We found this place of safety. At least it's safe now. We're selling paintings and sculptures to survive, but they all depict an alien world that none of us has ever seen, except our visitors, of course. Why is this happening? What goes through your minds when you create these things? Where is all this leading?"

"I just sit down and paint. I don't really think about it," says Travis.

"I don't give it much thought either," says Vera. "I just do it."

"Mama tells us what to do," says Edith.

"It's a pretend world," says Steve. "It makes me imagine that I'm there."

"It's fun," says Edith. "I feel good when I'm making it."

"Lena?"

"Ben directs me. Sometimes he gives me images and sometimes he uses words in my mind."

Ben nods.

Adriana says, "Why, Ben?"

After a moment of silence, Lena says, "They're homesick. Working on the sculptures and paintings helps them remember their own world. They're dislocated and frightened and this helps to stabilize them. They didn't realize that their promptings were a source of stress. They have tried to be respectful of their hosts. Us. At least that's what I interpret from the impressions that Ben is giving me. Is that right, Ben?"

Ben nods.

Lena says, "They can try to be more silent, but you have to understand that they are not corporeal in themselves. We are their bodies. The impressions we receive come from their dreams, their memories, their consciousness. They don't know if they can cut them off."

Adriana says, "Can the rest of us learn to communicate more directly?"

Lena says, "They're trying. They don't know if it's possible."

Walker says, "I don't know if we're going to come to any conclusions tonight, but since we're together, I'd like to bring up one other issue."

"Go ahead," says Adriana.

"I've noticed it on my trips into town. Sometimes I've managed to hear snippets of news from the outside. We've all assumed, I think, that the systems in place before the war have been recovering, that the world is slowly healing. But that doesn't seem to be happening. Things are not going back to the way that they were before; they're changing. Nobody seems to know exactly how or why. They're all waiting in anticipation of...something."

Adriana says, "Ben, do you visitors know anything about all this?"

Lena says, "They've sensed it, but they're not sure what it means. Nomad would know."

"Nomad said he would find us," says Sage.

"But he didn't say when," says Vera.

"That comes back to my question, I suppose," says Adriana. "In the meantime, while we wait, what do we do?"

"I think I can answer that," says Walker. "We get by the best that we can, just like the rest of the world seems to be doing. I don't remember what my life used to be like any more than the rest of you, but I have a hunch that things weren't any less confusing then than they are now. It's called the human condition, isn't that right, Sage?"

"Yes," says Sage. "That's what it's like in poems and stories."

Walkers says, "Poems and stories... We need some of those. Do any of you like to write?"

"I write sometimes," says Sage.

"Maybe you should keep a journal or something and write about all the changes," says Walker.

"I'll think about it," says Sage.

"I have something to say," says Louisa. "I think it's important."

"What's that?" says Adriana.

"I'm pregnant."

Adriana says, "What? Really?"

"Yes."

"We know," says Lena. "We all know. I mean the visitors."

Ben nods.

"This is wonderful," says Adriana. "We should celebrate."

Everyone gets up to give Louisa hugs and kisses on the cheek.

"We should have more music," says Adriana. "That's something I've been missing sometimes."

"The radio has a station or two that plays songs," says Travis. "I listen sometimes when I'm working on something."

"We should have *our* music," says Walker. "We've got painters and sculptors and writers. We should have some musicians too. Does anyone play?"

"It's hard to say," says Marcus. "I only found out I could read when I got a book in front of me. Maybe it's the same with the music. We may not know now, but we'd remember if we had the instruments."

"I suppose we could look around for some the next time we're in town, couldn't we, Travis?"

"Sure," says Travis. "Even if I don't know now, I'd like to learn to play something. Maybe the drums."

Walker chuckles. "I don't know if we could manage to get a drum set on the back of the bikes, but we'll see what we can do. In the meantime we could start with smaller instruments like guitars and flutes and harmonicas and so on."

Adriana moves over to sit next to Louisa. "How do you feel?"

"I get nauseated in the morning sometimes. I have trouble eating certain types of food."

"You tell us what you want and we'll try to get it for you," says Adriana. "Did you know about this, Smith?"

"She told me last night. I still can't believe I'm going to be a daddy."

"I just thought of something," says Celeste. "Is there any way that this baby could be part visitor?"

"No," says Lena. "There are only fourteen visitors, and they don't reproduce the same way we do. We're only vehicles; they're not part of our physiology." She pauses and then resumes. "It's possible that the baby might be able to communicate with them easier than we do, at least while it's in the womb. You've seen the situation with Ben. He has a closer link because he has less human education and training to impede the connection."

"I'm not sure I want that," says Louisa. "I want my visitor to leave the baby in peace."

"That's no problem," says Lena, "if that's what you want. Your visitor won't communicate with your child without permission."

"Thank you," says Lena.

VII

Weeks pass.

Fish proliferate in the strait, and Marcus has become an accomplished fisherman. He goes out almost every day with various partners and brings back enough fish to provide protein for everyone.

Sage, Travis, Smith, Celeste, and others who have had the time and inclination have cleared a large patch of lawn between the blue house and the russet cabin, have prepared the soil, and have planted carrots, potatoes, onions, tomatoes, cucumbers, pumpkins, beans, asparagus, beets, lettuce, and broccoli. They go out every day to tend the young plants, eliminate weeds, and watch for pests.

Walker and Travis continue their roughly one-a-week forays into town, although they stagger the specific days so that their patterns will not become too predictable. The paintings and sculptures sell briskly and fetch good prices, at least as good as the post-apocalyptic market situation will allow. Hailey sends most of them on to a contact on the mainland, from which the profits come back in the form of requested supplies as well as cash.

For music, Walker and Travis have managed to procure and bring back two classical guitars, a ukulele, a flute, a harmonica, and a pair of bongos. The basement in the blue house has been designated the music area. Vera and Celeste have a modicum of expertise with the guitars, and Travis has latched onto the bongos, practicing at every opportunity. As for the rest, various people try them out, but nobody else seems to already know how to play.

Louisa and Smith have become betrothed, as have Celeste and Lena. Marcus and Sage are in the early stages of a relationship. At Walker's request, the adults convened a special meeting to discuss sexuality within the family group. He was concerned that because everyone was already so intimate with each other these special isolated relationships could be a cause for discord. He wondered whether there might be a need for guidelines or limitations. After much discussion, the consensus was that whatever happens, happens, and the decision is between the people involved alone; however, for the sake of harmony, physical acts of affection will be performed in private.

Besides the continuing sculpture sessions and playtime outside, Celeste and Lena have begun homeschooling Edith and Steve in reading, writing, math, and other subjects.

And so time passes. They fish; they plant; they create art; they interact; they play; they learn. Meanwhile, as Walker and Travis glean from the news they gather whenever they go into town, the world systems around them wallow in confusion and uncertainty. There is a modicum of government, a modicum of security in the form of regional militia, a modicum of electrical power and water supply, and a modicum of transportation services such as trains, boats, and a few functional vehicles. Progress in bringing things back to an approximation of what normal used to be is excruciatingly slow. The war decimated the population and infrastructure, true; but also some sort of viscous lassitude in the collective human psyche is impeding reconstruction efforts. Nobody really knows why.

* * *

One afternoon shortly after Walker and Travis return from dropping off art and picking up supplies in town, a tall thin young man with long disheveled hair and a week's worth of beard wanders in from the main road. He pauses at the top of the path to the white house, where Edith and Steve are playing in the side yard. When they spot the stranger, they freeze momentarily and then run around the house and go in through the back door.

Celeste emerges and approaches the stranger. "Hello."

"Hi."

"I don't think I recognize you. Are you looking for someone?"

"My name is Jeremy Carter."

"Hello, Mr. Carter."

"I... I, uh... I'm looking for an old man and a boy on bicycles who turned into this driveway."

"Do you know these people?"

"Not exactly. I followed them from town."

"Why?"

"I'm looking for... Maybe I should talk to them."

"Just a moment." Celeste returns to the door and calls Edith. "Go quickly and call Walker and Adriana. Ask them to come here right away. Tell them it's urgent, but tell them not to run or act alarmed."

Edith bolts across the lawn and runs off down the driveway.

Celeste engages Jeremy in small talk. Within five minutes Adriana and Walker arrive.

"It's you!" says Jeremy.

"Do I know you?" says Walker.

"No, not personally. I saw you at Hailey Benford's shop. You're the one who's been bringing in all that amazing artwork of alien landscapes. I love it. I can't afford to buy it, but I spend a lot of time studying it before it gets sold. It's almost obsessional, the hold it has on me. I can't get enough of it. I'm an artist myself, but I've never been able to capture the mood and feel and details of a place like these paintings and sculptures do. Are you the artist?"

"No I'm not," says Walker. "Why didn't you ask Ms. Benford about the works?"

"I did. She said she didn't know the artists personally and she didn't know where they lived. So I decided to find out for myself. What is this place? Is it some sort of artist's colony?"

"It's private property, is what it is," says Walker.

"I don't think so," says Jeremy. "I know this island. I was brought up here. These houses were empty before."

"What did you say your name was?" says Walker.

"His name is Jeremy," says Celeste.

"Jeremy," says Walker, "it's true that we haven't lived here long, but I've checked local regulations and we have squatter's rights. We live here and we've been maintaining the properties."

"I don't mean to be pushy or aggressive," says Jeremy. "I know a few other artists in town, and none of them come near to the expertise I see in the works that you bring to Hailey. I want to learn to do what you do. I want to join the colony and take lessons. I'll do anything: work in the kitchen, manual labor... I just want a chance."

Adriana says, "Jeremy, our artists would be flattered that you appreciate their efforts so much. The thing is, though, that we're not really open to new arrivals just now. We're full up. We don't want to get overcrowded or we'll hinder people's inspiration and productivity. You can understand that, can't you?"

"Of course I can, but..."

"Plus we have no one that offers instruction. We don't have the personnel for it. We've all known each other for a long time, and we're a tight-knit group. I'm sorry we can't help you."

"But I promise I won't be a burden."

"That isn't the point," says Adriana. "The answer is no. I'm sorry."

"You don't understand," says Jeremy. "My art is all I have. Without it I'm nothing. I bare my soul. I let out all the demons that have accumulated during these dark days. I use pencils, watercolors, oils, and all sorts of other mediums. I work hard, hours and hours a day. And yet Hailey won't hang my pictures in her shop. She doesn't think they're good enough. She says I need more practice. I've come to you for help. Don't turn me away."

"I wish we could accommodate you," says Adriana, "but we can't. Aren't there any teachers in town?"

"There are a few, but I find their work mundane and boring."

"That's too bad," says Adriana. "You might find more options on the mainland."

"I don't want to go to the mainland. I want to join *you*."

Walker says, "How did you get here, Jeremy?"

"I rode a bike. I left it in some bushes near the highway."

"Well, it's getting late," says Walker. "You'd better get on your bicycle and head back to town or you won't make it there before dark."

With a frantic and despairing expression, Jeremy looks to Walker and then to Adriana and then to Celeste. He draws in a breath as if he's going to say something, exhales, and stomps up the driveway towards the road.

Walker waits until Jeremy is out of sight before he speaks. "This could cause us trouble. I'm sorry. It seems Travis and I have become lax with security measures."

"It's all right," says Adriana. "Don't blame yourself. People are bound to find out that we're here. If all he thinks we are is an eccentric artist's colony, then it shouldn't pose a problem."

"Still, maybe we could talk about ways to make this place safer," says Celeste.

"Of course," says Adriana.

"And we can come up with some contingency plans in case we're discovered by the wrong people," says Walker.

Celeste appears puzzled. "Contingency plans?"

"For escape," says Walker.

"We *are* vulnerable here," says Adriana. "We wouldn't get far if we tried to run away on foot."

"I've been thinking about that," says Walker. "We can try to obtain a vehicle, although I think they're scarce. We could also find a few more boats and store them in the boathouse along with packs with emergency supplies. If we had a bit of warning we might be able to cross the strait and get away on the other side."

"That wouldn't be easy," says Adriana. "The strait has a strong current."

"I know," says Walker. "We might be able to make allowance for that. Marcus could make some trial runs crossing and see how it goes, at least."

"Of course. We can talk to him about it," say Adriana. She hesitates. "I'm going to go and let everyone know what just happened. Maybe you two should walk up to the highway to make sure that our unexpected guest has really left."

"I feel sorry for him," says Celeste. "People are confused these days. They're looking for reassurance, for community."

"I wish we could offer it to them," says Adriana. "It's just not possible. Not now. We don't know what's going to happen. We've just recently fled from danger, and we don't know that the danger has passed."

*   *   *

Two days later in the long shadows of late afternoon, Nomad arrives. However, he does not walk down the driveway but instead he hikes over the overgrown hillside from the ruins of the fire-decimated house that Smith and Louisa had found. He waits near the russet cabin until Adriana and Andy emerge onto the deck before he approaches.

Andy runs up to him wagging his tail. *Nomad! Nomad!*

"Hello, Andy." Nomad bends over and scratches Andy behind his ears, and then straightens up to shake Adriana's hand. "Adriana."

"Nomad. Why did you come in this way? The driveway would have been easier."

"I know. I wanted to talk to you first before I meet all the others. You've become somewhat of a leader to them; not just to your seven, but to all of them."

"I didn't plan it; it just happened."

"Of course."

"Come and sit. Are you hungry? Would you like something to drink?"

"Not now, thank you. Maybe later. The house is empty, isn't it?"

"Yes. Louisa and Smith have gone for a meal at the blue house. I stayed because..."

"You knew I'd come."

189

"Yes."

They sit facing the water on wooden chairs with tie-on pads. Andy lies down at their feet.

"Go ahead," says Adriana. "Tell me."

"The rescue has arrived."

"Have you had any success finding more crewmembers?"

"Not many. A few who were thrown farther from the wreckage in isolated places managed to land in humans."

"Where are they now?"

"They're on the ship. That is..." Nomad looks out at the sunlight sparkling on the water of the strait before replying. "What a beautiful world," he says. "Most of it, at least. I'm going to miss it."

"Are you sure you don't want a drink?"

Nomad shakes his head.

Adriana goes into the house and emerges with a glass of red wine.

After she sits down, Nomad says, "We've found a way to extract our people. They're in stasis aboard the ship. They're confused and disoriented. They'll need a lot of retraining."

"And the humans?"

"They're healthy enough physically, but they haven't regained their memories. I tried to explain what was happening to them the best I could and set them up in comfortable situations, but our specialists don't know enough about your species to do any more for them."

"Or for us."

"What can I say? We have to get our people back. We have to help them."

"So then we're... What? Collateral damage?"

"I wouldn't put it quite like that."

"But it *is* like that. You use us to save your lives, and then you take away the one factor that has kept us united, and you cast us aside."

"We can't leave our people here. They don't belong here. They belong with us. They need to be healed."

"Has this ever happened before?"

"Never."

"You've always managed to create your suits, as you call them, when you visit new worlds."

"Yes."

"How do you know, then, that you're doing the right thing? Have you heard of symbiosis?"

"I understand the concept."

"How can you be sure that it hasn't occurred here? We are diverse species who were separate, but now we need each other to survive."

"You can survive without us."

"Maybe. But it will break us and leave us incomplete. We can never go back to the way we were before you came. Did you ask your people before you extracted them?"

"No. They're damaged. They're not in their right minds. They cannot make such a choice."

"But you didn't try. You didn't even offer them the opportunity. And now, as you say, they're broken, as we will be broken. I want you to go back to your rescuers and ask them to reconsider. Tell them what I've said. You owe it to us to at least think about it further. We saved the lives of your people."

Nomad nods. "I'll do it. I'm happy to offer you this courtesy. But I can't guarantee what they'll decide."

"I understand," says Adriana. "At least try."

*   *   *

Walker finds Adriana on a bench at the edge of the bluff near the path leading down to the beach. He sits beside her without speaking.

The sun has set. Its lingering glow slowly dwindles in the west. Below, waves slap and suck on the rocks in rhythm.

"I hope they didn't miss me," says Adriana.

"They were fine. A few wondered aloud where you were, and I speculated that you wanted some quiet time alone."

"Nomad was here."

"I thought he'd be back."

"The rescuers arrived."

"Ah."

"They located other humans with alien visitors and... They extracted them."

"I thought that Nomad had said that would kill them."

"They found a way. Now they... They want to take our visitors from us and go home."

"I see." After a pause, Walker adds, "You're worried about that."

"Our visitors, guests, symbionts, whatever you want to call them, are what made this family possible. Mine enabled me to find the original members and then drew the rest of you to us. They keep us together. They cancel our differences. They make us more than our individual selves."

"So you're concerned that if they leave, we will no longer have what we have now."

Tears form in Adriana's eyes and trickle down her cheeks. "I'm not just concerned. I'm frightened. I'm terrified. If Nomad and his people do this, what will happen to us? Will it be the same, or will we lose our connection?"

"Did you share this with Nomad?"

"Yes. I pled with him to let our visitors stay with us. He admits that the extracted aliens are damaged. They're hoping to cure them but they don't know if they can. At least if they remain here they can be part of something whole and complete and wonderful."

"It has been wonderful, hasn't it? We don't have the memories so we can compare it with our past lives, but we can see it when we compare it with the people around us, in town and on the mainland."

"Yes. That's what I tried to explain to him."

Walker puts his arm around Adriana and pulls her close so that her head rests on his shoulder. "Maybe we can't stop them from doing what they decide to do," he says, "but we can relish what we have while we have it. We can love one another day by day, and maybe if we do it fervently enough and sincerely enough our spirits will remember it even when the visitors are gone."

"Do you really think that will work?"

"Look at it this way: we've been doing it until now and we know it's been the right thing to do. Don't you think it will continue to be the right thing to do, regardless of what happens in the future?"

"Yes."

"There you are, then."

"Should we tell the others about Nomad's visit?"

"What effect do you think that would have?"

"It would worry them."

"Can we do anything to prevent it from happening?"

"I don't think so. Nomad found us here. I think he could find us anywhere."

"Let's wait then," says Walker. "Let's wait and see."

"All right."

Andy, who has been silently lying next to the bench, whines and moves closer, so that he is curled up at Adriana and Walker's feet.

*   *   *

Nomad returns a week later at twilight.

Everyone, Adriana included, is in the blue house sharing a meal. Two tables are pushed together, and around it are mismatched benches and chairs.

They have finished their repast and are sipping wine and other drinks and chatting about community projects when Nomad enters.

The door opening unexpectedly shocks everyone into silence. When they see it is Nomad, everyone except Adriana and Walker greet him ebulliently and invite him to sit.

Instead, he stops after taking just a few steps and says, "It's time."

"Time?"

"Time for what?"

"What do you mean?"

"What are you talking about?"

Nomad looks at Adriana. "You didn't tell them."

"No," says Adriana. "I didn't think you'd be back so soon. I was hoping you wouldn't be back at all."

"You must have sensed the lack of realism in that attitude," says Nomad.

"What's going on here?" says Vera.

Adriana says, "Nomad's rescuers have arrived. They want to extract our visitors from us and leave. Nomad admits that the ones they've

195

already taken out of humans have been damaged and dysfunctional, but they want to do it anyway. I asked them to reconsider."

"You should have told us," said Vera.

"Maybe I should have," says Adriana. "I'm sorry. I didn't want to alarm you."

"What happened to the humans after the visitors left?" says Marcus.

"They didn't get their memories back," says Adriana.

Marcus asks Nomad, "Did they remember what happened after the visitors entered them?"

"Yes," says Nomad.

"That's all right, then," says Marcus. "We'll remember our family."

"It's not that easy," says Adriana. "The visitors led me to all of you. If they leave, we'll lose what we have in common."

"I don't know if that's true," says Celeste. "How could we? We've been through so much together."

"I see what Adriana's getting at, though," says Smith. "The visitors have given us something special. Now that we have them, we're somehow greater than we were. I think they should stay with us."

"It's not your choice to make," says Nomad. "They're not part of you; they're distinct entities. They have been using your bodies as suits, as vehicles to move around in. However, you have become redundant."

"Redundant?" says Walker. "That's a rude way of putting it. We saved their lives."

"I apologize," says Nomad. "I made the wrong word choice. But you have to understand our predicament. They're our people. We have to bring them home."

"What if they don't want to go home?" says Celeste.

"We know that they'll want to go," says Nomad. "Some more than others. Think of the visitor within Ben, for instance. His physical abilities are severely limited. It's not a viable vehicle for him. Isn't that right?"

Ben nods.

"And the one within Andy is not even in a human body. He has no way of communicating with most of you." Nomad leans over and scratches Andy's neck.

Andy barks and wags his tail. *Andy wants to go home!*

"Do you understand what I'm saying?" says Nomad. "You have to think of them, not just of yourselves."

"All right," says Adriana. "Let's think about them. I assume that you believe in freedom of choice for your people just as we do with ours."

"Of course," says Nomad. "But your visitors, as you call them, are not whole, not complete. They're damaged, so we have to make their choices for them."

"Are they more damaged than we are? Or have they simply lost their memories?"

"Besides memory loss, they lost certain other abilities, mainly having to do with communication."

"Do you mean the type of communication I use to communicate with Andy and Lena uses to communicate with Ben?"

"Yes."

"So apart from these defects they are intact?"

"Yes."

"Then why can't they make up their own minds?"

Nomad doesn't answer immediately. He looks from one to the other around the table.

"All I'm asking is that you let them choose for themselves," says Adriana. "If our visitors want to go with you, that's the end of the argument. But if they want to remain with us, how can you think of forcing them to leave against their will?"

Nomad says, "Do you realize that you would be condemning them to permanent exile? As soon as we retrieve our people, we're leaving and not returning, at least not in the foreseeable future. Your planet is too volatile, too violent."

"Of course living in exile can be harsh," says Adriana, "but only if it's involuntary."

"I think I had better have a seat," says Nomad.

Marcus grabs an extra chair from a corner and sets it next to Adriana's.

"Now what?" says Adriana.

"Just a moment," says Nomad, and closes his eyes.

Logs crackle in the fireplace. Sparks erupt into the chimney.

Marcus goes to close the door that Nomad left ajar before he sits down.

Outside, the wind picks up. Tree branches stir. Raindrops begin to patter on the roof.

Nomad opens his eyes. "That's it, then. I'm done here."

Walker says, "What do you mean you're done? We haven't..."

"Something's wrong," says Adriana. "You're gone from my mind. All of you. I can't feel you anymore."

"I can't hear Ben," says Lena.

Ben starts crying.

"What have you done?" says Celeste.

"What I told you I would do," says Nomad. "My crewmates have been rescued. You no longer serve as vehicles for them. You're free."

"Free?" says Celeste. "If this is freedom we don't want it."

"Bring them back," says Adriana. "Please."

"I can't," says Nomad. "They're being placed in protective stasis for the journey. Don't worry. We'll find a way to help them, to heal them."

"And what about us?" says Adriana. "What's going to happen to us?"

"I don't know," says Nomad. "You'll live your lives. Maybe your condition will improve in time. There's nothing more we can do. We can't take you with us; you wouldn't survive in our vehicle. And we can't stay here."

Nomad stands and heads for the door.

Adriana follows and grabs his arm. "Wait. You can't leave us like this."

Nomad pulls his arm free. He appears as if he is going to say something else, but then he turns, opens the door, and disappears into the darkness.

VII

The lights flicker, remain on, but become dimmer.

Ben continues to cry until Lena starts nursing him.

Marcus drops a couple more pieces of wood on the fire, and the glow from the flames increases.

Adriana sits back down.

"What do we do now?" says Travis.

"I don't know," says Adriana.

Andy pushes Adriana's hand with his nose; she absentmindedly rubs his neck.

"We can still stay together if we want to," says Walker. "For safety. For protection. For comfort. As a community, like before."

"It won't be like before," says Adriana. "It can't be."

"So we'll do it the human way," says Walker. "Imperfectly."

For a time they sit in silence as rain drums heavily on the roof.

"Ben's fallen asleep," says Lena. "I need to put him to bed. Come on, kids. It's still pouring. Go ahead and make a run for the house."

"I'll hold an umbrella over you and Ben," says Celeste.

After Celeste, Lena, and the kids have left, Louisa says, "I'm tired too. I think I want to go to bed."

She and Smith leave sharing an umbrella.

"We've all had quite a shock tonight," says Walker. "Maybe we should have a good night's sleep and then get together and talk in the morning."

As she is leaving, Adriana pulls Walker aside. "I've always been confident until tonight. Now I don't know what to say, what to do."

"That's all right," says Walker. "It's going to take us time to adjust. We shouldn't do anything hasty. We have to take the time to get to know one another as people."

"What if we don't like each other as people?"

"Don't worry about that," says Walker. "We've been through some difficult times together. We already have a lot in common."

Adriana smiles wanly, calls Andy, and leaves.

*   *   *

The following evening, Marcus slips into the room Sage shares with Vera, awakens Sage, and signals her to meet him in the hallway.

"What is it?" says Sage.

"Will you come for a walk with me?"

"It's late."

"I know. I have some things on my mind."

"All right."

A half-moon illuminates the path down to the beach. Marcus and Sage stroll silently hand-in-hand until they reach the foot of the bluff, where they sit on a large driftwood log. It is high tide, and waves lap the pilings of the dock. The water shimmers with flecks of silver.

"What is it?" says Sage.

"Adriana's right," says Marcus. "It's not the same anymore."

"I know."

"I thought about it, and I want to leave."

"Leave? Where will you go?"

"I don't know. I only know that today everything was different. I could see that people were trying to be kind, to be inclusive, to be unselfish, but it wasn't working. It was forced."

"There's been a big change. You have to give it time."

"That's what I told myself at first. As the day progressed, though, and things got more and more awkward, I realized that I only have to give it time if I want to. And I don't want to. They're not coming back, Sage. We're on our own. I don't feel that I fit in here anymore."

"What will you do out there all alone?"

"Not alone I hope. I want you to come with me."

"Me? But I can't... I mean..."

"Didn't you feel it too? We're not a community anymore. We're a group of individuals. We don't need to ask permission. We can go where we want and do what we want."

"I need to think about it. When were you planning to leave?"

"Now."

"Now?"

"Yes. Now that I've decided, I don't want to wait. We can take a boat and row across to the peninsula. If we like it we can stay there. If not, we can move south. We're in no hurry. We can do anything we want."

"If we're in no hurry, why do we have to leave now? Why can't we wait and say goodbye to the others?"

"Because I don't want them to persuade us to change our minds. I know this is right, and I want to follow through with it while I have the resolve. If we stay, I know it's going to get worse. I know it. I don't want to wait around for it."

"All right," says Sage. "I'll go with you."

After a prolonged kiss, they draw apart and Marcus says, "I'll go back to the house with you so you can get your things. Try to fit what you need to bring into a small pack."

"What about you?"

"I'm ready. My pack is here, and I've also brought some water and enough food for a few days."

"You had this planned?"

"Yes. The only thing I couldn't plan is the decision you'd make. For that I could only hope."

While Sage is gathering her few belongings, Vera stirs in her sleep and turns over, but she doesn't wake up.

Soon afterwards, Marcus and Sage are moving away over the water; their wake creates an ever-widening funnel of silver on the dark water. Sage hopes to catch a glimpse of the cabins, but they are set too far back from the bluff.

"Goodbye," she whispers.

*   *   *

You pour a brandy, go out onto the deck, get comfortable on a lawn chair, and ruminate.

As usual, Andy follows you and lies down at your feet. Since the visitors left, he has accompanied you everywhere, and although he can no longer communicate with you mind to mind, you feel that there is still a bond between the two of you. You understand each other, and your affinity provides solace despite the ongoing mood of melancholy that has pervaded the community. Community? Is it still a community or merely an aggregate of individuals? Last night Marcus and Sage took one of the boats and crept away without farewells and without telling anyone where they were going. A piece broke apart from the whole. Until they left, you had been struggling to retain the concept of community, both in your own mind and in your remonstrations with the others. Now you feel broken. For too long you have identified with the collective consciousness, and you find it difficult to disassociate from that image. You hope that it is an isolated incident and that the rest of the group will heal, but you don't have the confidence that you used to that this will prove to be true. You realize that you were one of the forces that kept it all together, but you have changed. You used to be strong, decisive, confident, assertive, and optimistic; now you are weak, hesitant, insecure, frightened, discouraged, and doubtful.

What do you do after suffering such a great loss? How do you recover? You realize that it was otherworldly intervention that drew in your family in the first place. It was supernatural in that it was beyond the ability of humans alone to create. Now that it is gone, you have joined the rest of the humans on the planet in the isolation of your individual minds. The difference is that most humans have never had the opportunity to experience anything else. They live out their lives in blissful ignorance. To be given it and then have it snatched away... That's what hurts.

You hear footsteps. Louisa and Smith come out onto the deck and sit.

"Hi," says Smith.

"It's a beautiful evening," says Louisa.

"Yes," you say. "How are you two holding up?"

"We're fine," says Louisa. "It was a surprise that Marcus and Sage left."

"In a way it was inevitable," says Smith.

Abruptly a surge of fear rushes up your spine and explodes in your head with a tingling sensation. You become convinced that Louisa and Smith are planning to leave too. Your heart pounds furiously. You want to take a sip of your drink, but you are afraid that your hand will shake. You manage to blurt out, almost in a whisper, "Why do you say that?"

"Things have changed, haven't they?" says Smith.

"Are... Are you two thinking of leaving?"

"Oh no," says Louisa. "We like it here. It's beautiful. It's a wonderful place to raise a child."

"There is something, though." says Smith.

Louisa leans forward. "We're going to be our own family now: Smith and me and the baby."

"Of course," you say. "I'm so happy for you."

"Thank you," says Louisa. "What we're trying to say is... We've loved having you here, but we feel we'd like to have the cabin to ourselves now."

"What?"

"Please try to understand. We still love you, but we want this to be *our* family home. Just the two of us. And then the three of us."

"You're throwing me out?"

"Of course not," says Louisa. "We have no right to do that. We know what you've done for us. For all of us. It's a request. We want to live alone for awhile."

Your first reaction is indignation, and your first impulse is to give an incisive retort. *I'm not going anywhere. Go off and find your own damn cabin.* But you know you won't say that. You're desperate to hold as much of the group together as you can. At least they want to remain in the area. At least they're not sneaking away like...

Your second impulse is to let yourself go, to weep and to sob. You don't do that either. You feel no ill will towards Louisa and Smith and you don't want them to feel bad. Scant days ago people would have moved from house to house with impunity as needs warranted. Now...

You swallow the rest of your drink. "I'll pack my things."

"You don't have to go now," says Louisa. "There's no hurry."

"It's all right," you say. "I might as well."

You give each of them a hug and briefly rub Louisa's belly. You then go to your room and throw the few belongings you own into your backpack. When you're ready, you hoist it on, and you and Andy head up the road towards the blue house.

Only when you're sure that you are out of earshot of the inhabitants of the russet cabin do you break down and cry.

IX

Walker and Travis are cycling into town with the last paintings for sale. No one is creating anything new. Celeste, Edith, and Steve have left the final landscape sculpture incomplete. Everyone is bereft of inspiration. In Vera's words, "Maybe I'll eventually start painting again, but it will be nothing like it was before."

The highway is empty of vehicles as usual. Walker and Travis proceed at a moderate speed, side by side, to avoid the risk of an accident that might damage their cargo.

"I have something I want to say," says Travis.

"I'm listening," says Walker.

"I'm getting tired of being told what to do."

"What do you mean?"

"When you brought up the trip into town this morning, you didn't ask me if I would go. You told me. You took it for granted that I'd do what you say."

"I thought you enjoyed the ride."

"That's not the point. I'm a free individual. I want to make my own decisions."

"I certainly didn't mean to order you around, Travis. I think we're all in a process of adjustment now that the visitors are gone."

"I've heard that a lot these past days," says Travis. "It's no excuse."

"Of course not, and I'll try to be more respectful from now on."

"Will you let the others know too? I'm growing up. I want to be treated with respect."

"I'll tell them."

They ride in silence for awhile in the cool shade of the towering evergreens on either side.

"What's going to happen to us?" says Travis.

"We'll be all right."

"Marcus and Sage left. What if others leave? I don't want to be left alone like I was when Adriana found me."

"We won't let that happen. I promise. You can count on me."

By now they have reached the outskirts of town. They park their bicycles outside Hailey's shop, untie the bundles of paintings, and go inside.

When Hailey comes into the shop from the back, she says, "Oh, it's you. Do you have some new pieces?"

"Yes," says Walker, "but these might be the last. We're going on hiatus for the time being."

"Maybe it's just as well," says Hailey. "Some people were in here recently. They showed me photos and asked if I had seen the people on them. You weren't one of them, Walker, but he was." She points to Travis.

"Me?" says Travis. "Why?"

Hailey says, "I don't know, but they didn't seem to be fans of your artwork. They insisted they were old acquaintances, but they were stern and serious. They seemed like officials of some sort. If I were you, I wouldn't want them to find me."

"What did you tell them?" says Walker.

"Nothing. I told them nothing. They never mentioned the paintings. I don't think they associate them with you. But if they came in here and asked me, they probably asked everyone. It might be a good idea to stay out of town for awhile. I hope you have enough supplies to manage."

"We'll get by," says Walker.

"I can advance you the payment for the new pieces," says Hailey. "In fact, if you want, you can wait here while I gather some supplies for you to take back."

"That's kind of you," says Walker.

"I figure you'll need food more than money if you're going to lay low."

Hailey returns within an hour with bags full of groceries and household items. "If you need anything, Walker, you should come alone next time. I'm sorry, Travis, but it might not be safe for you. In the meanwhile, I'll start a rumor that the artist's colony has moved on to another location."

"Thanks," says Walker, "for everything."

"We've all been through tough times," says Hailey. "We have to watch out for one another. Take care."

*   *   *

Celeste awakens just after dawn. The morning is still, quiet, and chilly. Beside her, Lena continues to sleep deeply with a slight snore. In the home-made wooden crib next to Lena, baby Ben seems to be sound asleep too.

Celeste wonders what woke her up. Regardless of the cause, she has no desire to go back to sleep, so she rises, puts on jeans, tee-shirt, sweater, and slippers, and goes out into the front room, where the final landscape sculpture spreads out unfinished. At the large picture window she pulls the curtain aside just a crack so she can observe the colors of the lightening day. The sky over the tops of the evergreens is deep blue and cloudless. In the confusion of the past days, one thing that has remained constant is the loveliness of the scenery. It has helped to stabilize Celeste. Some of the Bible verses that the nuns taught her even pop into her mind from time to time.

The earth is the Lord's, and the fullness thereof; the world, and they that dwell therein.

The heavens declare the glory of God; and the firmament showeth his handiwork.

He hath made everything beautiful in his time.

She is not sure why these words have begun to come to her. Sometimes she wonders if the indoctrination of the nuns has contaminated her appreciation of pure beauty. Sometimes she muses if she might unknowingly be a Christian. The thought somewhat frightens her, but not so much that she is unable to use the words to amplify the feeling she has when the pure beauty of nature strikes and stuns her.

But now... Who is this?

Someone is walking up the driveway from the direction of the highway. Tall, thin, disheveled hair, scraggly growth of beard... It's that would-be artist Jeremy Carter who came looking for classes. What would he be doing here so early? If he came by bicycle, he would have had to have left town long before first light.

He stops at the gate and looks towards the house.

Celeste defensively closes the curtain.

This isn't right. Adriana and Walker were definite in their refusal to accommodate his request to stay. What does he want now? Is he coming to try again?

Celeste considers that it won't be difficult to tell him no this time. Nobody is creating artwork anymore. It won't be a lie to inform him that the artist's colony has disbanded.

Lena and the children are all asleep, and Celeste doesn't want them to be disturbed, so she decides to go outside and quietly persuade Jeremy to leave.

She slips on a jacket, unlatches the door, steps out, and closes it behind her.

"There you are!" says Jeremy.

"Of course," says Celeste. "Why wouldn't I be?"

"I thought you might have all left. No one came into town last week."

"Could you keep your voice down please? There are people asleep inside."

Ignoring her request, Jeremy says loudly, "So you're all still here - your colony, your group?"

Celeste stops a few feet from him. "Jeremy is your name, isn't it?"

"That's right."

"I thought we made it clear that we couldn't give you art lessons."

Jeremy avoids looking Celeste in the eyes. "It wasn't right. You should have helped me."

"Maybe we should have. It's too late now, though. None of us are painting and sculpting anymore. Things have happened. Personal things."

"Where are the others? Are they still here?"

"What others?"

"The people who spoke to me. The ones who told me I couldn't stay."

Celeste frowns. "Go back to town, Jeremy. There's nothing for you here."

As she turns to leave, Jeremy grabs her arm. "They're here!" he shouts. "They're here! She's one of them!"

Celeste jerks her arm out of Jeremy's grip and runs. She has almost reached the door when shots are fired from the cover of the trees. She falls, and her head hits the concrete walkway heavily. Blood seeps out from the holes in her jacket and from under her head.

Lena opens the door and sees Celeste. Before she can scream or take a step towards her, there is more gunfire, and Lena falls next to Celeste.

One of the shots has shattered the front picture window. A uniformed militiaman lights a makeshift firebomb, and throws it inside the house.

The supervisor from the facility that had held Adriana runs out waving her arms and shouting. "Wait! Wait! What the hell are you doing?

I said firing was a last-resort option. We need them alive. Stop!"

The militia man who threw the bomb says, "They were displaying aggressive action, ma'am."

Behind him the wooden structure erupts into flame. First fire takes hold of the furniture, curtains, and alien sculpture in the living room, and it spreads quickly to the rest of the house.

The supervisor turns and shouts, "Cease fire! Hold your positions. Do not fire without my orders, do you understand?" To Jeremy she says, "You've done your part. Go home."

He is staring in shock at the bodies and the burning house.

"You heard me," said the supervisor. "Get out of here."

"You haven't paid me yet," says Jeremy. "You promised me compensation."

"You'll receive what you're entitled to," says the supervisor. "Right now, though, we're in the middle of a classified, top-security situation that's none of your business. And a word of warning: don't say a word of what happened here to anyone. It won't go well for you if you do."

"I won't."

They stare at each other for a moment, and then Jeremy backs off and hurries quickly up the track towards the highway.

To the militiaman who threw the bomb the supervisor says, "You go on back and wait with the others."

"I did what I thought was necessary," he says.

"I know," she says. "For now, wait for orders. If anyone tries to run, capture them, but without violence. I'm going in to talk with them."

"Alone?"

"Yes. Don't worry. I'll be fine."

By now a roaring conflagration is consuming the remains of the house. The supervisor backs away from the heat, and then heads down the driveway towards the blue house.

*   *   *

Semi-awake and feeling slightly nauseated, Louisa is lying beside Smith on their bed in the russet cabin when she hears the gunshots.

She shakes Smith. "I thought I heard shooting. Go and see."

"Huh?" Smith rubs his face, shakes his head, gets up, and goes to the window facing inland. "There's smoke coming from up the road. It could be one of the other houses."

"They've found us," says Louisa. "They're attacking. What do we do?"

"We've got to get out of here," says Smith. He grabs his backpack and starts throwing in a few essentials.

"What about the others?"

"It looks like it's too late for them."

"Shouldn't we wait and find out if we can help?"

"What can we do? We've got no weapons. And remember we're not alone. We've got to think of our baby. What will they do to it when they find out you're pregnant? We've got to protect it. Come on."

Louisa touches her stomach pensively and then hurriedly dresses.

When Louisa and Smith are ready, they go out the sliding door to the deck.

"We'll head north across the hillside," says Smith. "We'll stay off the roads. We can do it."

They have made it no more than halfway across the recently-mown lawn when two militiamen armed with rifles step out from behind trees.

* * *

In the blue house, Walker is already awake and has gone downstairs when the gunshots sound. He runs around to the bedrooms rousing Adriana, Vera, and Travis. Within minutes they are all dressed and downstairs.

"The white house is burning," says Walker.

"What about Lena and Celeste and the kids?" says Vera.

"I don't know," says Walker.

"We have to go see," says Vera. "We have to help them."

"No," says Adriana. "We've got to get away."

"What if they're caught in the fire?" says Travis.

"They're not," says Walker. "We've been attacked. There were gunshots."

"We know who it is, and we know how ruthless these people can be," says Adriana. "The way to the highway is blocked. You three run to the dock and get the boat ready. I'll try to take a look at what happened at the white house and then follow you."

"No," says Vera. "You can't..."

"I'll be fine," says Adriana.

After they go out the back door, Adriana says, "Go on now. I'll be right behind you. Andy, you go with them."

Andy ignores the order and stays with Adriana.

Walker, Vera, and Travis stay within the shelter of the stand of evergreen trees that parallels the path to the beach until they reach the bluff. They then follow the top of the bluff until they come to the zigzagging path that leads to the dock. They are about halfway down the path when two militiamen step out of the boat shed and take aim at them.

*   *   *

Adriana circles around the blue house to the front and runs up the driveway, Andy beside her. She momentarily thinks of clandestinely making her way to the site behind trees and bushes so that she can remain unobserved, but her grief and despair has gotten the better of her. She doesn't give a damn anymore. It's all over. Whatever she thought that she was building for the well-being of her so-called family is in ruins. The hell with the invaders. Let them do their worst.

She spots the supervisor approaching, the same supervisor who captured and deceived her before. This woman has pursued her relentlessly for hundreds and hundreds of miles and won't leave her alone. Adriana has an overwhelming urge to hurt her, to kill her, but then she thinks of her loved ones in danger and attempts to veer around her nemesis.

The supervisor grabs her. "Wait! You don't want to go there."

Adriana tries to wrench free.

Andy is barking furiously.

"Listen to me," says the supervisor. "You don't want to see what's there. Trust me."

"Why should I trust you?"

With that, the supervisor falls silent but does not let go.

X

Adriana waits in a beige room with bars on the window. She sits on the bed with a couple of pillows propped up to cushion her neck and back. Behind the bed is a table full of instruments with

219

which they have been testing her. Adriana's mind is blank. All the questions have been asked and the answers given. Now she is in limbo. She cannot even summon the mental energy to wonder what will happen to her.

The door opens and a nurse enters. "The supervisor will see you now."

Adriana rises and follows her down the hall, waits while the nurse opens the supervisor's door, and enters the now-familiar office.

"Sit down," says the supervisor.

Adriana sits in the chair opposite the desk.

"How are you?" says the supervisor.

Adriana doesn't know how to respond so she says nothing.

The supervisor says, "We've been able to definitively ascertain that the entity that you called a visitor and we referred to as an invasive alien is no longer within you. We're going to let you go."

When Adriana remains silent, the supervisor continues. "We're not pressing any charges for your flight or even for the way you handled the employees of this facility when you escaped. You'll have to sign a nondisclosure agreement, though, promising not to speak of this facility or what you went through in it to outsiders. If you break that agreement, you'll be severely punished."

Adriana finally speaks. "Where are the others?"

"They're gone. They've been released. I don't know where they went. Louisa and Smith left together. Walker and Travis left together. Vera left alone. You're aware that these are not their real names, aren't you?"

"It doesn't matter."

"Adriana isn't your real name either."

"It is now."

"You have a past. Don't you want to know what your name used to be?"

"No. If I can't remember it, what's the point?"

The supervisor sighed. "We tried to restore your memories but were unsuccessful."

"What happened to Celeste and Lena and their children?"

"They died."

Tears trickle down Adriana's cheeks.

"The men who fired the shots and threw the fire bomb were way out of line. They have been relieved from their positions in the militia and are undergoing retraining in a secure facility. I'm sorry that this happened; I really am. We took extreme action, yes; but we were trying to contain what we perceived as a threat."

Adriana wipes her cheeks with her hands.

"I'm not an inhuman monster. I'm trying to do what is right. My name is Patricia, by the way. People call me Patty. I thought you should know that."

The supervisor pauses again. When Adriana still doesn't reply, she says, "There's one more thing." She presses an intercom button on her desk and says, "Bring him in."

The nurse enters leading Andy on a leash. When Andy sees Adriana he barks loudly and starts forward but is stopped short by his restraint.

Adriana lets out a joyous sob. "Take that off him, please."

The supervisor nods.

Andy leaps onto Adriana's lap and frantically licks her face.

* * *

Once she and Andy are outside, Adriana has no idea where to go. She begins walking and recognizes that she is on the same path she took when the supervisor set her loose to search for her family. It happened only a few months ago, but to Adriana it seems much longer because it is at the extreme limit of her memory.

Passing by a large rock, Adriana says, "This is where I first met you, Andy, do you remember? You were hunting a lizard."

Andy barks and wags his tail.

As she walks, Adriana recalls finding Celeste, and then Travis, and then Marcus, and then Sage. She misses them all, not with the visitor-induced telepathic awareness of their presence, but with the emptiness that all humans feel when someone that you love is absent.

When she reaches the city center, Adriana is more cautious. Many of the streets are still full of rubble and shadows, and the inhabitants slink away with glum, suspicious looks or watch her dispassionately from windows. She really has no idea where to go. It's late afternoon, and she doesn't want to be outdoors after dark. She supposes that she should find a house, many of which must be still empty, especially in the outer residential areas. She considers their mansion on the hill, but she has no desire to return there. It would be a long walk, and she would feel intimidated in that enormous place all by herself.

But wait. What about the house with the lighthouse-like tower by the sea where they first met Vera? It's smaller, cozier, and not far from where she now is. Perhaps there's a bit of food and drink left. Right now she'll settle for tap water in exchange for the comfort of being surrounded by protective walls so she can think and grieve in peace. She can sequester herself in that beautiful isolated place until she figures out what to do.

After she makes that decision, Adriana feels lighter in spirit. She can't quite summon up a smile, but at least she is slightly less distraught.

Andy seems to sense the change. He barks and leaps about.

Adriana stoops to scratch behind his ears. "Come on, Andy," she says. "Let's go."

As she ascends the seaside hill with the fading colors of sunset still aglow to the west and more and more stars illuminating the darkening night sky, Adriana remembers the night that she, Celeste, Travis, Marcus, Sage, and Andy hiked up to the house on the bluff and found Vera waiting for them with a feast prepared. What a wonderful celebration that was! They were all so hopeful and united and full of love.

Now she and Andy are alone and return in ignominious defeat.

Adriana hesitates at the gate. She wonders if she has made a mistake in coming here. She wonders if the memories that awaken will deepen her despair.

It is too late to second-guess her decision, though. If the place overwhelms her, she will leave in the morning.

She unlatches the gate, and after she and Andy are inside latches it again. During the walk up the long drive weariness sets in.

The front door is unlocked. When she opens it, the light is on in the entrance hallway. Could they have neglected to turn it off when they left so long ago?

Andy runs ahead into the dining room and starts barking.

Adriana follows slowly, not comprehending at first what is happening. But then there they all are, sitting around a table laden with food and wine:

Vera, Walker, Travis, Louisa, Smith, and even Marcus and Sage.

Adriana is overwhelmed. She sobs. Tears flood her cheeks. She thinks she might pass out.

And then they are all around her, hugging, kissing, comforting, all talking at once and explaining how they made their way there to that place. Hints of images and ideas, emotional tugs, seemingly unrelated decisions that funneled them inevitably in one and only one direction.

Home.

End Notes

John Walters is an American writer, a Clarion West graduate and member of Science Fiction Writers of America, who recently returned to the United States after living abroad for many years in India, Bangladesh, Italy, and Greece. He writes science fiction and fantasy, thrillers, mainstream fiction, and memoirs of his wanderings around the world.

You can find his website/blog at:
http://www.johnwalterswriter.com

Other Books by John Walters

The Love Children: A Novel

It is the mid-1970s. The Summer of Love and the Woodstock Music Festival have come and gone. Into the atmosphere of cynicism and doubt following the wild optimism of the youth revolution the Love Children, raised from birth by benevolent aliens, come home to Earth. Sexually free, telepathic and honest to the extreme, they are appalled to find that the world they left behind is full of darkness and deceit. As they set about using their extraordinary powers to bring light and unity back to their world, they run up against a sinister alien force intending to keep it in darkness.

The Fantasy Book Murders

After a famous fantasy writer is murdered in his castle-like mansion, two unlikely investigators discover a pattern of similar murders suggesting a serial killer. They begin to research the killings, starting with the most recent and working backwards into the past. Danger mounts as they uncover the backgrounds of the victims and the truth begins to resemble the fantasy writer's most bizarre and horrific fiction.

Caliban's Children

Content is being siphoned from libraries and being replaced with half-truths and lies. Weather, time, and distances are distorting like images in a funhouse mirror. People are discovering the ability to morph into animals. At first it all seems idyllic and magical until a dark power begins to manifest itself, assert control, and demand obedience.

Ethan is a university student caught in the midst of a kaleidoscopic confusion he cannot understand. After journeying into the wilderness seeking answers, he realizes he has to ally himself with the beasts of the Earth and venture into a bizarre, mutating, peril-filled city to rescue his lover and attack the source of the evil.

www.ingramcontent.com/pod-product-compliance
Lightning Source LLC
Chambersburg PA
CBHW020911160726
47993CB00005B/1914